THE BLACK SWORD

MARSHA LYN

Cover design by Tatiana Villa
Interior design by Veronica Yager

I would like to dedicate this book to all eleven of my children.

Especially to my son David for always telling me how great my book is

and that everyone needs to read it. Also my dear Analise, my youngest

with the red hair and brave soul who inspired the Princess Analise in

The Black Sword. *I thank you all for your parts in my life,*

I would not be me without you.

CHAPTER ONE

Rolling over the top of the mountain the fog crept down the draw as quiet and gray as a stalking cat. It fed itself on rocks and trees as it started to fill the valley below. I knew my time was limited, with this new development it was going to be hard to see in that thick fog. I needed to speed up, sit it out or chance getting lost in the fog. I hitched my pack up, took a deep breath and started down the trail that lay before me moving fast, twisting and turning around boulders and trees. I could hear a small stream tumbling down the slope to the left of where I was descending; it must be feeding the small lake I had seen from above that was being slowly consumed by the encroaching fog. This valley was not my destination; I was passing through and I had to climb the opposite ridge. I did not know if my destination lay there, but it was in that direction I just needed to outrun that fog.

I had been traveling since I left home early this morning before anyone was awake, up and around doing all the things my family does on week day mornings. I chose a week day because my dad was less likely to come after me when he had everyone else to get moving. I knew they would not be happy but they knew I could take care of myself because they had taught me. We had lived out here in the mountains forever as far as I knew. My sisters and I were all homeschooled, any kind of regular school being too far away for us to attend. I'm Trevor Lee Dawson thirteen years old, old enough to be on my own. I have my dads coloring with black hair and bright blue eyes, broad shoulders and narrow hips even at thirteen. My sisters, Lily Jane is eleven, Rose Ellen is eight, Daisy Jean is five and Violet Marie is two, Mom likes flowers and middle names. They all look like mom with long thick blond hair and bright blue eyes and I knew when they grew up they would have the same curves. Each of my sisters has their own patch of ground with their flower growing on it around the log cabin we live in. I'm kind of surprised I don't have a flower for a middle name since dad insisted on Trevor for my first name. Dad takes care of the Oregon Natural Park in northern Oregon where we live in a big log house with a red front door and a big brass handle.

I had headed out from there about four this morning and knew I was well out of the park by now. I had raided the pantry as well as stocking up on trail food and water. I had a change of clothes, extra socks, boots, gloves, hat and a weather resistant coat rolled up in my fiber sleeping bag. I had my pocket knife in my pocket with some water proof matches, a hunting knife in its sheath and my thirty-eight in its holster on my belt. Guns were rare but dad had given it to me and taught me how to make bullets and I didn't want to leave it. A small shovel and saw were strapped on my pack; extra ammo I had made for the gun and a small cook pot were in it, and a hundred and forty-seven dollars in the lining of my boot. I was saving it for a rifle but figured I'd probably need it and would never find a rifle anyway; maybe this is why I was saving it. I also had a small hunting bow we used when hiking. We were all used to hiking; the nearest town is twenty-five miles from the house. If we want to go anywhere we have to hike out and if we want to take anything we have to carry it. We don't have horses since it's not easy to feed them in the mountains. Nothing gets left on the trail so you better be sure you want it enough to carry it. We all have packs even Violet for her favorite doll of the day and a change of clothes in case she pees.

Most of us could shoot and hit what we aimed at except Violet and she was working on it. We used longer bows when we were target shooting. We knew our way in the woods and mountains, guided by the stars or the earth if visibility was limited. I was fairly certain I could get where I was going I just didn't know where that was. I've had an itch right in the middle of my back where it can't be reached for a couple of months. Then the dreams had started dreams of walking, moving, traveling, and always north and toward the coast. The urgency started to get to me day and night that I needed to move. Mom commented on me fidgeting when I was supposed to be doing school work, she thought it was just being a boy and she'd send me outside to do some work like chopping wood for the fire or just play around. A couple of weeks ago I heard a voice, the sweet soft voice of a young girl, only it was in my head. We have enough girls around the house I know what they sound like. This girl was asking me to come. To hurry because she needed help, she didn't say where, I would know. It never occurred to me to talk to my dad, he always taught us to take care of our own problems and for some reason I felt it was a secret I needed to keep besides it's a little strange to hear a girl in your head. It made me nervous and felt dangerous to even think about telling anyone anything. I was being called; I was being pulled toward this voice only I could hear for whatever reason. I had no choice and I was on my way.

The fog was filling the valley quickly as I stepped down the mountain. The trail was clear, probably a game trail and if I was lucky I might catch a rabbit or squirrel to supplement my supplies and make it last longer. The fog; cool and damp reached up to embrace me the closer I got to the bottom. It was strangely quiet and unreal. I could not see a thing except gray and gray swirls as my feet cut through the fog. I needed to make a decision, try to continue on and hope I don't get lost or worse fall over a cliff. Or should I sit it out despite the urgency in the girl's voice. The fog crept up my legs twining around my boots then up my calves to my knees. Moving ahead I felt sluggish as I became aware of what was happening with each step and the fog encased me further. I kicked out and it swirled around then settled back around my legs firmer then before. I swatted at it with my hands and it clung to them and started to creep up my arms. I was getting scared and realized I was making mewling sounds and a cold chill shivered down my spine, how do you fight fog when it starts to attack you? I realized the more I struggled the worse it was going to get so I stopped fighting and tried to relax. How was I going to get out of this; dad had never taught me about fighting fog! I had to think my way out of this. I dropped my arms and the fog dropped away, I slowly and carefully dropped my pack and hit the quick release on my sleeping bag. I had decided to sit this out inside my sleeping bag. It gently unrolled along the uneven ground the open mouth at my feet. The fog was swirling around as if it had lost track of me; it had puddled at my feet and I knew if I made any quick moves it would be back up my legs tighter then ever. In slow motion I lowered myself to the ground and started slowly wriggling into my bag. This agitated the fog and it swirled around me tightening then loosening as I forced myself to relax. I was breathing hard as I wriggled further into my bag pulling my pack with me. It seemed to know something was up and caressed my face tightening around my neck and face and I moaned. Even though I was getting more scared by the minute having the fog around my face was terrifying me. I forced my head to drop and relax, it was one of the hardest things I have ever done but it worked. I slipped the rest of the way into my bag pulling my pack in with me and pulling the drawstring. I reached into my pack grabbing my extra shirt I jammed it into the small hole at the top, I had to keep the fog out. It was going to get hot and uncomfortable but I figured I wouldn't suffocate in a fiber bag. My body slumped in relief, it felt a lot safer then being out in that fog that wanted to creep up my legs and arms and tighten around me, that didn't feel safe at all.

I lay in my bag my breath making it hot and I started to get lightheaded and my body was trembling. I thought I was hallucinating when I was lifted off the ground but I wasn't. I was wrapped up tight and rolled around then slammed into the ground a couple of times and I screamed knowing no one could hear me. Then it squeezed the bag as if the fog wanted to squeeze the breath out of me. Thankfully I had dragged my pack in and it protected me since the fog couldn't get purchase around me. I was picked up again and instead of being slammed against the ground again there was the sensation of floating. I was terrified; I didn't know what kind of fog this was to be able to do this to me and who was responsible for it? I hoped with fervor it wouldn't throw me off a cliff, and then I passed out.

Chapter Two

I woke up a while later and took a deep breath, god it smelled bad in this bag. I wondered how long I had been out. The small hole the shirt had been stuffed into had sunlight streaming into it. I thought; well I lost my shirt and that was some creepy fog. I heard a beating rushing sound and birds cawing, I couldn't quite place it so I decided I should find out what it was. I moved and it hurt, I was so stiff, that fog really did a number on me. Moaning with stiffness I sat up and shinnied out of my sleeping bag and it ripped down the side startling me; that was weird it was a fairly new bag. Dad insisted we have excellent gear as our lives may depend on it in the mountains where we live. I looked around in astonishment, and then I stood up and looked around. Amazingly I was perched on the flat top of a short mountain on an island in the ocean just off shore of somewhere and the noise was the cawing of dozens of Sea Gulls circling over head. I could see the mainland from where I was standing. I was having trouble processing everything I was seeing; my face itched so I absently rubbed it confused and wondering how I got here from the valley I had been in. I was shocked to realize I was rubbing hair. What the hell! Dad frowned on cussing. But hair on my face deserved cussing. What the Hell! I put both hands up to my face and my shirt ripped down the back. I was completely confused; this is a new shirt, what is going on? I pulled my hands away from my face to look around me and realized my hands stuck out of my shirt a good four inches. Still more confused I wondered how my shirt could have shrunk that much in fog. I took deep breaths through my nose to calm myself, rationally I knew it wouldn't. I looked down and my jeans were way to short and way too tight and my boots were not even on my feet. My hair fell over my face, it was long and greasy and I had to pull it back over my shoulder. I looked in my sleeping bag and found my boots and compared them to my feet. They were way too small. My belt was wrapped around my gun and knife in the bottom of what was left of the bag. I sat down and gazed out at the ocean and wondered how long I had been in that sleeping bag. I was in shock, nothing made sense and I couldn't move. I no longer heard a voice in my head and I was worried about what could have happened to the girl.

I sat amid the cawing of the Gulls looking out to sea when my stomach rumbled. Absently I pulled my pack over to me and searched for something to eat. It was in good shape when compared to my sleeping bag. The perishables were dust long ago and did nothing to help me know how long I had been here. The bird shit on my bag told me as much though there was a lot of bird shit. I found some Jerky that was serviceable if not palatable. The Jerky made me thirsty and all my water bottles were empty. Is there water that can be drunk on this rock I wondered? That is what made me move, the thirst. The pants were unbearable so I unbuttoned them, the shirt also. I wrapped the rags of what was left of my coat around my feet to keep from cutting them on the rocks as I walked. My sleeping bag was a total loss so I left it as well as the unusable stuff in my pack and my boots after removing the laces. My bow was dry and brittle so I tossed it with my bag. Sliding my knife into my pocket I put my empty water bottles, gun and belt in my pack and picking it up went in search of water. I found a small stream tumbling down slope as I came around a curve in what I called a trail and was really a scratch in the rock. I took a small sip and it seemed fine so I took a larger one. I didn't die so figured it was OK and felt great relief. I continued to make my way down slope along the stream, it seemed the easiest way. There was a small pool at the bottom and I was thinking bath, I smell as bad as a herd beast. First I drank my fill and I had to fill all my water bottles. There was an outlet into the sea but it would take a while for it to filter if I took a bath and I needed the water to drink.

I leaned over to fill my first water bottle when I saw someone in the water. Startled I jerked back drew my knife and crouching looked carefully around. I was panting hard from fear. I don't know where that wild man I just saw in the pool went but he wasn't going to sneak up on me again. My daddy didn't raise any fools. I crouched there a few seconds calming myself and then bent over I started looking for footprints so I could follow this guy and find out what he is up to and what he wants with me. He might know how I got here and if he was responsible for me being here he was going to tell me why I was here and where here was. I searched all around the rocks and in the sand but I found no prints so I went back to the pool thinking weird things are happening here, I need to find a way to leave this place. I drank my fill then I filled my bottles keeping an eye out all the time for the wild man then I stripped and slipped into the pool. I scooped up sand from the bottom of the pool to scrub with. I scrubbed every inch of my body and was rinsing my hair that had grown a good foot when I chanced upon the wild mans reflection in the water again scrubbing at his hair. I was shocked into immobility as I realized that man was me. I put out my hand and touched my reflection on the water gently caressing back and forth making the water ripple seeing the boy I should be and wondering how this man could be me. When the water stilled the wild man was back and stillness settled over me. How can this happen? How much time has passed? I flexed my arm and the muscles rippled beneath my skin that was milk white. I was not undernourished just pared down to good muscle and little fat and my deep tan was gone. If I had been in that sleeping bag as long as it took to grow a foot of hair I should have starved. Like I said, some weird things were going on here. How can I look grown up and feel thirteen. I sat stunned in the pool, not really knowing what to think.

A cloud passed over the sun and I felt a shiver through my body. I finally roused myself, got out of the pool and dried in the sun unable to figure out how I got here. Needing something to do, I started figuring out what to do about clothes instead. My hair kept falling forward so I combed it with my fingers and then I pulled it back and tied it with a piece of leather. Hair out of the way I got out my extra pants that were way too small and slit them up the side with my knife and cut them off just above the knee. I cut the legs off the pants I had been wearing slit them up the sides and laid them in the slits in the sides I had made in my first pair. I poked a bunch of holes along both sides and then laced the whole thing with leather thongs I had in a pocket of my pack. They fit pretty good considering I was so much bigger. I had a light blue blanket with a zigzag pattern on it of darker blue. I slit it about six inches across in the middle then four inches down the front. I laced up the sides with my boot laces and slipped it over my head; it would do for a shirt for a bit. The boots I had left were just way too small but my money had still been tucked in the lining and I slipped it into a pocket in the pants. I left the rags on my feet since I had no other option. Thank god my hat still fit. I checked my gun which had been well oiled when I had put it in my holster so it was fine and the ammo was wrapped in oil cloth so it was dry. I was hungry, it felt like I hadn't eaten in years and I probably hadn't when I considered how old I could be. I couldn't even fathom how whatever happened could happen to me, so I didn't think about it. It was time to figure out how to get to the mainland and find out where I am and more important when, I had been on this island way to long.

I started along the beach picking my way to save my feet. I walked all the way around the island and ended up staring at the mainland from the point I had started from. I turned and looked inland, there was the mountain and there were a few scant trees around its base. I decided there might be something there I could use to make a raft or something I could float on. I knew I could not swim as far as the mainland looked. My dad being big into survival had taught us the basics of swimming but there were not a lot of places to swim in the mountains. The mountain lakes were snowmelt and so cold you couldn't stay in very long or die from hypothermia. There was no ocean swimming though I knew about tides, I knew I would not be swimming across that stretch of ocean. I started walking into the scraggly trees noticing small branches littering the ground and hoping to find something a little bigger. I walked through the entire copse of trees finding only small branches but a lot of them so I started collecting them and making a pile on the mainland side. I sat and stared at the pile I had made, it was getting dark and I had resigned myself to spending another night on this island. As I stared I started to visualize a woven mat, a mat made of branches and I started to weave. I cut the longer branches with the saw I had on my pack, it was still in good shape.

As it got darker and there was only a sliver of a moon I was afraid I would have to stop when I remembered my waterproof matches. I took some of the smaller sticks I couldn't use and used it for kindling. I found some short thicker branches and a few pieces of logs. I started the kindling then fed in the rest and found I had enough light from the fire I had made to continue weaving. I made a basic mat then built on top of it interweaving branches to hold it all together. I worked tirelessly all night energized by the thought of getting off this island. By morning I had a mat three feet thick by about six feet long and four feet wide. I left a shallow hollow in one end to put my bag and clothes in and planned to hang my feet off the other end to kick to the mainland. It was kind of a makeshift raft and it should work as long as the whole thing doesn't come apart and float away or sink to the bottom me along with it. I tugged, pulled and even kicked it a few times and it seemed sturdy enough. I studied the current and realized the tide was going out the same time I realized how tired I was. I ate the last of my jerky, drank a bottle of water, shoveled sand over the fire then lay down using the mat as a pillow and went to sleep.

As I slipped into a deeper sleep the dreams came, dreams of my family and my home in the mountains a long way from where I was. There were horrible soul tearing dreams of cries and screams, smoke and fire traveling the distance in time and space to reach my eyes and ears. As I woke they stood out in stark pictures in my mind and in my despair one pair of small blue eyes stared at me from the darkness. I knew my family was dead except for one pair of blue eyes. She had been hidden, my youngest sister. My silence had not kept them safe as I had hoped and worse then I had ever imagined had come to pass. I didn't even know why. I had left for a voice that I didn't hear anymore and was sure I needed to keep secret. I had left them to their fate and I had been no help to them then or now. I lay there on that beach and wept bitter tears. I wept for dad who I know tried valiantly but vainly to protect his girls by killing as many as he could. They took him first thinking victory would be easy with him gone. The number of dead on the ground around him told a different story, so many dead were heaped around him it was like a wall of dead. I wept for my mom whose babies were gone so there was no longer a reason to live. She stood in front of her burning home and died with her hands clutched to her breast and head bowed though I knew she believed in no god. There was a great number of dead around and in front of her and her quiver was empty with each and every arrow finding a mark. I beat the sand and screamed my rage the tears burning my face. The blood that flowed from her many wounds and from under her hands told me she had fought as the warrior I knew she was to protect her family. My sisters had a great number of dead lying on the ground around them proving they had fought well. They had fought back to back as they were taught and I having learned with them and fought them knew they were unbeatable unless overwhelmed by numbers. The number of dead around them was so high you could barely see over them. Very few men walked away from the fight that day their heads hanging low and not one without a wound. They had brought many men expecting resistance but getting a war. I hoped they felt shame in their hearts for the children they killed. But I knew they didn't, those children had stood and made their own lives mean something. They had taken on full grown men and even though they had not won would never be forgotten for the fierceness of the fight. They were still dead. I wept for my sisters and the flower beds they were named after seeped in their blood as they fell. I wept for lost innocence and lives that would never be lived. I screamed because I had loved my beautiful sisters and I couldn't protect them. I beat the sand and cursed the sky and the girl voice who had taken me away to end up on this cursed island. Blue eyes swam before my eyes pleading and I gave pause, one lived, one had been hidden and I would never rest until I found her. My family had hidden her before they died. I don't know where she is probably wasn't there anymore but she was alive and I would find her. I would also find those who had walked away after killing my family and whoever sent them, they were all going to die. I would bring the war to them and it would be a war they would never remember because they would be dead. I pledged on the blood of my family to see their blood flow, watch it seep into the ground and watch the crows pick out their eyes. On my knees gazing into the heavens I swore I would find those blue eyes that belonged to my baby sister Violet. I rose to my feet in fury searching the tide and found it was going in. I stripped my clothes off and shoved them into my bag being sure I had everything worth saving and threw it onto the raft. I pulled it into the water the cold shocking my bare skin but I was fevered by my need to seek, find and take revenge for my family. My eyes saw only red and I wanted to kill and kill some more. I was driven by my rage and the rage made the crossing to the mainland easier and quicker then I thought possible.

CHAPTER THREE

I stepped onto the mainland and a woman called out my name as loud and clear as a dinner bell in my head, I stumbled and almost lost the raft. On my knees in the water I looked around and saw no one near. Regaining my footing I pulled it upon the beach then I sat in stunned silence as she spoke to me.

["At last, you are awake at last!"] She said, ["I have been waiting ever so long for you to escape that accursed island."]

I was simply too stunned to answer. Who was this person talking in my head, she sounded as if she knew me. Was this the girl I left my home to go find and instead I got waylaid on that island? My whole family except one was killed and I didn't even know where, much less when I am, or who she was and she was back in my head. I was angry. Following dreams was a dangerous thing to do I was finding out.

["Analise, I am Analise."] The voice more cautious now said.

["Why did you never tell me your name?"] I asked my anger in my voice.

["I was afraid; I was a little girl and didn't know who to trust. When you came into my mind it was too much for me to hope you could help me and you were so far away. I now know you were meant to help me and the more you know the better it is for all of us."] She said.

["I came into your mind?"] I asked surprised.

["Oh yes, in the dreams. I knew I could trust your blue eyes but I was still afraid."] She said.

["My eyes, you saw my eyes? Why would you trust me because of my eyes?"] I asked now confused.

She sounded confused as she answered, ["Because only people with blue eyes can be completely trusted. Don't you know how rare that is? Or how rare blue eyes are?"]

I thought of dad, mom and my sisters and their bright blue eyes. Everyone I knew had blue eyes and for the first time I wondered if there was more to living in the mountains away from people then I thought. What did dad know that I didn't? Why didn't he tell me?

["He knew you were a treasure that in the wrong hands would be used against good even though you are incapable of evil. In the wrong hands good can be twisted to serve evil with horrific results. Even your anger and desire to kill those who hurt your family is righteous and you would be allowed to exact revenge. Blue eyes stand for truth and righteousness, it is inbred and a path you must follow."] She said.

["What color are your eyes?"] I asked.

["Emerald Green with gold fire."] She replied.

["Do you know where my baby sister is?"] I asked angry again.

["Yes."] She said.

["How long has it been?"] I asked.

["Twelve years, two months, sixteen days."] She replied.

["I am twenty-five years old today and yesterday I was thirteen."] I said shocked and badly shaken.

["It would seem like that to you, to us it has been an eternity. We have waited long for you to wake. We could not touch you on the island; all we have been doing is waiting and staying alive. We need you. You are our salvation."] She said urgently. ["You must come to us."]

["Just who are us?"] I asked.

["You must come."] She said, and was gone.

I rose and pulled my clothes out of my bag. I was dry after that conversation so I got dressed. I wondered how I was supposed to find Analise and her friends, people, subjects…. Whatever. I heard a faint whisper: [you will know.] I was dazed and disoriented it had been over twelve years, I was twenty-five. I had people to find, people to kill I didn't have time to go north as I pulled on my pants. I am twenty-five. I heard that whisper again; [you will, they are here, come.] I guess I need to monitor my thoughts if she could hear everything I thought. How could I be twenty-five years old? Maybe I could put up a door and she would have to knock to get in. That's not a bad thought, I thought, as I pictured the front door to the cabin. I'll have to think on that, having a girl/woman just walking into my head anytime was a little disturbing and could be embarrassing. I was in shock; I was twenty-five. I pulled on my blanket shirt thinking about placing a door in my mind and how would I go about that, when I heard a knocking sound. I looked around and didn't see anything knocking or anything to knock on. What the hell, what is it now.

When there was a knocking sound again I said, ["What?"]

["How did you do that?"] Analise said

["What?"] I asked, though I had a pretty good idea what she was talking about.

["The door! You have a red door in your mind with a brass knocker on it. I could not hear you; I had to knock to talk to you. How did you do that?"] She asked

["Red door, huh!"] I said as I thought of the red front door at home with its big brass knocker.

["Yes!"] She cried, ["That's it, where did it come from?"]

["Memories,"] I said, ["It's a privilege, opening that door, don't abuse it."] I said shortly and closed the door.

Well now that was a neat trick. I thought and it happened, I would have to think on what else I could do. I was on that island twelve years, I couldn't process it. I hoisted my pack, and then I thought blue eyes. No one has blue eyes; I was going to stand out, eyes were the first thing a person looked at. I sat my pack down and started going through all the pockets thoroughly. I thought of my dad for some reason and the day he was fiddling with my pack when I walked into the storage shed just before I left. What had he been doing? I paused, my dad has been dead twelve years and it took my breath away. I lifted the big flap on top and ran my hand over the inside. Something about what he had been doing was here. I felt a flat oblong object and saw the loose stitches at the bottom; I worked them out then slid the object out. I just looked at what was in my hand then focused on the writing on the package in my dad's hand. "Trevor, son," he had written, "In need remember to always make them brown. We will always be watching over you, all love Dad."

I was shocked; my dad had written on this and hidden it in my pack just before I left; so he knew more then he let on. Shit, my dad was dead had been dead twelve years and he was reaching out and protecting me even now all these years later. Dad, what did you know? I thought. Why didn't you tell me something? I was only thirteen or twenty-five but it would be nice to have some useful information whatever age I am. I opened the package and there were six pair of brown contacts floating in fluid bubbles. Dad, what did you know? I had read about contacts so I opened two bubbles and with a bit of effort inserted them into my eyes. It stung like crazy but with a lot of blinking and tears they settled in. With my long black hair, beard and brown eyes I would not stand out at all I thought. Unless everyone went clean cut in the last twelve years, I sighed, shouldered my pack and started up the beach heading north. Why north, I had no idea but it felt right and she said I would know. North it was. It would be all the better if I found someone I could kill when I got there. My rage had dimmed in the shock of her voice in my head and the number of years lost but I was more determined then ever and it was a cold determination. She had said they were there, did she know them? I shook my head in frustration, I felt uninformed, lost, angry and out of my element and that was a dangerous thing to be.

CHAPTER FOUR

I trudged along in my rag shoes and blanket shirt trying to avoid the worst of the rocks. I followed the beach sloughing through the sand with my head down. As I came around a group of boulders I ran right into a guy sitting on the beach in my path, he was staring out into the ocean looking sad enough to make even the clearest sky cry sleet and rain.

Taking a few steps back my concern about clean cut was completely alleviated; this guy was down right scruffy with a beard, scraggly hair and dirty hands. I noticed he had been digging in the sand near the stand of boulders behind him and I wondered why. I stood observing him with my thirteen year old mind and wondered what could make a man so sad that he sat in the sand and stared at the ocean looking lost but somehow determined. I thought of my family and decided maybe we had something in common. I cleared my throat and he glanced up at me.

"Move along stranger, this is a private party" He said then turned back to the ocean.

I sat down a few feet away and stared out at the ocean searching for what he saw. It was beautiful, it was beyond beautiful. I had not noticed the ocean before when I was trying to get off the island angry and wanting nothing except to kill someone. During the conversation with Analise I was too shocked and preoccupied to notice the biggest presence I have ever seen or felt as it surged at my very feet.

The waves were big grey swells rolling in and breaking in huge sprays of white water all along the beach, some bubbling up and over like froth in a kettle and all of it pounding onto the beach as if it was trying to reclaim it. Pounding out a drum beat of waves that this beach is mine no one has a right to it except me. The colors were intense from dark grays and deep blues, greens, turquoise, translucent pearl with diamonds sprinkled all through. It rumbled with a deep voice demanding acknowledgment of its presence and might, its ability to pound rocks to sand and affect the turning of the earth. My eyes rose and I studied the sky, it went on forever iron gray and blue with strings of white and light gray clouds reflecting the ocean below. Through the last rays of the setting sun the gulls cawed, weaved and dove dipping up the fish that rode in the swells that rose from the deepest depths. My eyes settled on that point of infinity where sky meets ocean and goes on forever, I could see sky and ocean with the sun setting into the deep waves shooting an array of reds, oranges and yellow as it broke through the clouds the second it sank below the water. My heart beat a quick tempo, my head sang and my body trembled at the beauty of all I saw. Suddenly I saw a bright deep green flash on the horizon and the light began to fade. I gasped and rocked back where I sat with my mouth hanging open.

The man spoke startling me, "First time?" He asked.

"Yes." I said. I had forgotten all about him in the thrall I was in.

"A person forgets how beautiful it is when life takes over, it was a pleasure watching it with you." He said.

"Are you from around here?" I asked.

"I used to be, just stopping by on my way through to another place." He said.

"Me too," I said.

He got up and said, "I got to be moving on." He took off and then dropped a long leather coat at my feet then he took off his boots and dropped them on top. He nodded his head as if to say; wear them well. I was too surprised to speak. He walked to the waters edge and kept right on walking, when he was about waist deep he dove under a wave and came up swimming. He could really swim and he was plowing through the waves at a speed that would take him wherever he was going quickly. I stood and watched him disappear into the dark of the great ocean and I wondered why a man would do that and where he was going.

I looked down and picked up the boots, they looked about right. I tried them on after taking off the rags and they were a bit loose so I did one wrapping of rags around my feet and they fit perfectly. I tried on the coat and it fit really well. What a great gift from a total stranger and I can't even thank him I thought. It was full dark so I moved up near the pile of boulders above the high tide mark. I rolled up in the coat using my bag as a pillow and I was soon asleep soothed by the waves crashing upon the beach.

Chapter Five

I was woken up by insistent knocking on the red door in my head. I was going to have to teach this woman some manners starting with patience. I dulled down the knocking and rolled over to see what looked like a grave where the man from last night was digging. I jerked back and rolled the other way and stood up looking down at the sand that had obviously been disturbed, and then rocks had been piled upon it. It looked like a grave even standing up, a somewhat small grave, a child or maybe a small woman. I looked out to the ocean and saw nothing except waves and I got a chill. What did he mean; he was on his way through to another place? There were no islands in sight so unless he is a really great swimmer he was only going to go down into the water. Damn, I thought, but then what could I have done for a stranger I didn't even know. I looked down at the sand I decided to assume it was a grave; I sure as hell wasn't going to dig it up to find out. I picked up my pack, pulled on my hat, turned north again and started walking. I needed to think about this and that woman needed to stop knocking and wait. My boots kept time to the insistent knocking in my head, acceptably soft now, as I walked up the beach.

I was having a hard time getting my mind around the possibility that a person I was just talking to was now dead because he wanted to be. That he had swam into the ocean until he could swim no more and just let go of life. I thought about my family and the great fight they fought for life even if only one survived. What would make a person want to die before their time? He must have had a good reason, but I could think of nothing that would make me want to die. So what made him want to die if in fact that was what he did? This was getting me no where. I decided to find out what Analise wanted, and then I decided I would ask her what she thought about it. I opened the door and there she stood in all her frustration.

["It's about time you got up!"] She stormed.

["Why would someone kill themselves, do you know?"] I asked and blew the wind right out of her sails. She just sort of collapsed in on herself.

["Oh my god Trev, are you OK? I know your family is gone but we need you so badly. Please don't do anything until we meet and I can see and talk to you in person."] She said.

I was astounded, she thought I might kill myself but she gave me one reason, loss of family. I wondered who was in that grave and if that was the reason he chose to die.

["I met a man who swam out to sea. He left a grave on the shore. He gave me his coat and boots then just swam away. I don't know why anyone would do that, I couldn't think of a good reason and you gave me one, family. Maybe he lost his family."] I said.

["Oh Trev that's awful, I am so sorry you experienced that. He just swam away?"] She asked.

["Yes and I have been trying to figure out why. He may have lost his family, he did leave a grave. I lost my family and all I want to do is kill the people who killed them not kill myself. Could he be a Silkie?"] I asked.

["I thought they were myths. Do you think they could be real?"] She asked.

["I don't know, but why not? I talk to you in my head, how normal is that?"] I said. ["Why were you knocking?"]

["I don't know, doesn't seem important now after what we just talked about."] She said. ["You didn't have boots or a coat?"]

["No, I grew out of them on the island, so I made due with what I had."] I said.

["What does that mean?"] She asked.

["Not important,"] I said.

["Hurry Trev, things are getting scary here,"] she said.

["What does that mean?"] I asked, but she had softly closed the door. I trudged up the beach on my way north. I guess I should have hurried but its hard walking in sand and I didn't want to leave the beach yet, so I trudged in sand listening to the beat of the ocean.

I should have thought I would run into trouble. I mean why waylay me on an island for twelve years and then let me walk calmly north to my destination and the woman who keeps talking in my head. Here I am walking along thinking about why someone would choose death over life instead of revenge. When I should have been thinking about people who would want me dead and I should have been taking evasive action. At least I should have been covering my tracks not trudging, but that may be just what saved my life that day.

A group of guys, big mean looking men accosted me a few miles later. They asked if I had seen a guy on the beach acting funny. I told them about the guy sitting on the beach staring out at the ocean then swimming away. They nodded their heads and said maybe the ocean had done their job for them, then went on down the beach.

I kept trudging north. Analise knocked a bit later and said she had heard there was a force of men out looking for me and I should avoid them at all cost. Someone was trying to stop me from going north, probably the same people who dumped me on the island twelve years ago. I didn't know what else they might have up their sleeves but I didn't want to find out. I figured the beach was not the best place to stay so I headed inland. Within a few paces I came to a rocky surface that went on as far as I could see, winding around and through copses of trees and sand. I back tracked kicking sand over my prints then headed for some coarse grass with a few trees scattered about and some big rocks. I could still hear the ocean pounding in the background as I waded into the grass, after a few steps I swung up into a tree, it wasn't as easy as I remembered as my thirteen year old self but I managed. I looked down and my prints looked like I had headed into the trees heading due north. I crawled out onto a branch and dropped onto a rock, hopping from rock to rock up another tree then a bit more rock hopping till I came to the trail of rocks heading off to the north east roughly the way I needed to go. I knew I wouldn't fool the thugs for long but they didn't look to smart so I knew I would get at least a head start before they figured out where I went.

I needed to think about what I was going to do if they caught up to me; I knew what they were going to do would probably be painful. I started thinking about my door in my head and visualizing a door ahead of me between two trees that would lead me to the place Analise was. I heard noise behind me and caught a glimpse of men coming at a run over the rocks, they had figured out my ruse, quicker then I thought they would. I need to remember not to underestimate people, even unwashed thugs. I turned back to my path and there before me between those two trees was a door, large, thick and heavy wood with a big metal circle pull handle. I stopped short, hearing yells closing in behind me, what the hell; then I thought I'll take a chance with the door. I pulled it open and stepped through into blinding sunlight on white snow full of crystals. I whirled around as the door thudded shut behind me and disappeared. I was in a valley surrounded by the biggest mountains covered in snow I have ever seen. I stood looking at a huge castle sitting on top of a swell in the valley with a narrow road twisting and turning up a steep incline and disappearing into a huge gateway that had a huge gate closing it tight.

Chapter Six

I was pretty sure I was north, it felt like north. I wondered if this was where Analise is, and is this her home or what? It sure was big and I didn't know how to get in or if I wanted to get in except it was really cold here. I didn't know what to expect, there seemed to be plenty of people who wanted me to not do what I was doing, whatever that was and were more then willing to stop me. But then why would I come here if it was dangerous? A small door opened in the big gate and a horse trotted out pulling a sleigh. It was a big black horse and a small sleigh with an even smaller person sitting in it with a red cape ruffed about the face with white fur. As horse and sleigh approached I discerned it was a woman driving, she had long red hair blowing in the breeze from under the fur ruff. As she got closer I could see the big smile on her face and as she got even closer I could see it reflected in her green eyes flecked with gold fire. She drove up and stopped beside me.

"Hello Analise." I said, "It's good to finally meet you."

She grinned and said, "Get in Trev, its freezing. Are those short pants you are wearing?"

"I made due," I said as I climbed in beside her.

She examined me closer and asked, "Did you make those clothes? Not the coat, surely, did you?"

"Not the coat, or the boots, they are from the man on the beach." I said, "It is freezing Analise."

She nodded in understanding then laughed, wheeled the horse and sleigh around and headed back to the castle. We were inside quickly after she gave the horse to a handler. There was a big fireplace I backed up to and was soon warm again. Going from the ocean to a mountain winter in the blink of an eye was a little disorienting. I was glad I was where I was backed up to this fireplace in this land of snow. Analise had gone off to store her coat and she now returned carrying a small round blue marble box with a lid that screwed on. She handed it to me and I looked at it curiously holding it on my out stretched hand.

"You don't have to hide who you are here." She said.

"OK," I said cautiously, still more confused.

"It's to put the brown contacts in when you take them out of your eyes." She explained pointing to the box.

"Oh, I'm supposed to take them out?" I asked, "How does this help?"

"Have you never worn contacts before? Where did you get them if they are not yours? Never mind for now, you take them out of your eyes by gently pinching them between your fingers and put them in the box. It has fluid in it that keeps them from drying out and you can reuse them. There is a bath being drawn for you in your room and clean clothes laid out. Let me show you where to go, we can talk later at dinner. Everyone will want to know what you say and it will save you repeating yourself." She pulled me along as she walked and talked, even demonstrating how to take out contacts. It looked harder then putting them in was.

She opened a door into a large room done in different shades of blues. There was steam rolling out of another door and a woman I took to be a maid rushed out and said the bath was ready and everything lay out. Dinner was in one and one half hours so I could rest a bit. Someone would be at my door at that time, and I should be prompt. I stood there holding my new contact box looking at the maid scurrying around amazed at everything.

Analise laughed and said, "Go on, you look a mess. Get cleaned up and we'll see you soon."

I nodded and she left in a whirl of green dress I happened to notice looked really good on her, with the maid following her out looking at me curiously. I went to the steaming room and there was a tub big enough for three people full of hot water. There was plenty of soap of all different kinds, a mirror and a razor with soap and brush. I had seen my dad shave many times, how hard can it be I thought? I stripped off my dirty make shift clothes dropping them into a pile I stepped into the tub and sank into the water relaxing for the first time since I woke up on the island. I just sat and reveled in hot water; I had never seen let alone sat in this much hot water ever. I dozed a bit then decided I had better wash if I was to be on time for dinner. I submerged holding my breath for as long as I could then came up out of the water taking huge gulps of air pushing my hair back.

There were a lot of soaps and I figured out there were some for hair, some for face and some for body. Why you needed so many soaps I didn't know but I liked the hair one so I used that for everything. I got out and dried off on the biggest fluffiest towel I ever saw and wondered how they got them so soft, they sure had not been hung on a line to dry. I approached the mirror and found a brush; I brushed my hair and tied it back with a piece of leather, I decided I liked it long. Then I decided I would feel better with my own eyes looking back at me, and took out the brown contacts and put them in the little blue box, it worked real neat though it hurt if you pinched too hard.

I looked at my beard in the mirror. It was intimidating; I had decided I didn't like it. It had definitely grown more and it itched incessantly, but how to go about getting it off. I called up an image of my dad after he came back from a week hunt and then I picked up a pair of scissors lying on the table. I cut the hair off as short as I could get it then soaped up the brush and sopped my face good. I gingerly picked up the razor heartily wishing my dad was here and missing him enough for tears to trickle from my eyes. I wiped them away and continued to shave determined to do him proud even if he couldn't see me. I only cut myself three times and they were shallow cuts that stopped bleeding quickly. I applied a hot cloth to my face and as I lowered it I finally saw myself for the first time and recognized it was me. My blue eyes did not lie to me, could not lie to me, this was really me. The small blue eyes floated into my mind, where is my sister? I had to find out.

I went to my pile of clothes and realized I could not bear to put them back on. I stood with the towel wrapped around me, some how I knew it would not be proper attire for dinner. That's when I realized there was an entire set of clothes laid out on the bed. The bed was also big enough for three people, but what interested me were the clothes. There was underwear which I slipped into feeling immensely more comfortable. A pair of black pants made of a fabric I had never seen or felt but was soft and really strong, maybe a type of leather. They were a perfect fit. I pulled on a pair of heavy socks then a pair of soft supple boots made for being indoors. Last was a shirt, blue silk with long sleeves; a pullover with black leather ties and tails to tuck. Oh yeah, there was a belt with a silver buckle, not too big with what looked like a sapphire inset in it. There was a full length mirror in the corner and I stood gazing at myself, was this really me?

CHAPTER SEVEN

All I could remember was the gangly youth who left my parents home following the voice of a young girl in trouble. She had turned into a young woman, as I had turned into a man. Weird, I thought as a knock sounded at my bedroom door. The Raven, I thought, knock knocking at my bedroom door. Then I looked twice as the door swung open to reveal a large black man dressed all in black.

"My name is Dorian," He said with a smile, "I insisted I be the one to escort you to the dinning room. Anyone else would ask too many questions you would feel obligated to answer then have to repeat. Are you ready to go to dinner?"

"As ready as I'll ever be." I said, and he laughed, as we walked I asked, "Could you answer some questions for me?"

"Yes, as much as I can." He said.

"Where am I?" I asked.

"You truly do not know?" He asked, and I shook my head no.

"So you did come by the doors," He said, "You are in the land of Clarion at Castle Clarion owned by the clan of Clarion whose line Analise is the last female that still walks the high ways."

"Analise Clarion?" I asked.

"Yes, to you that is who she is. To us she is Princess Analise Marisa Lafayette Clarion of Clan Clarion heir to the throne of all lands and in grave danger though she will yet laugh." He said as we walked.

"Who do we dine with this evening?" I asked.

"Royals, members of the court, interested persons, and persons interested in meeting you to learn how you can be used and exploited." He said.

"Which one are you?" I asked.

Dorian laughed heartily then said, "You are young but the later will be sorely disappointed. I am not of the royals but a trusted family friend and member of the court. Analise is my Goddaughter and I would protect her to my last breath."

"That is a noble calling protecting Analise. I am sincerely glad that you do, and you are concerned about me being here and how I will affect her. I think I understand where you are coming from." I said.

"You understand nothing, but you must and quickly. You have talked much with her in your youth and she has waited, not willing to act until you came back to her. You were a long time on the Island of Dreams, things have changed much. There is a prophecy that says;

> Blue eyes will be there all your days,
> to protect and lead you in all your plays.
> Move not one step until he paves the way.
> Sleep he must, wake he will,
> and strong he will be to make the kill."

He said. "Analise has been waiting for you because of that prophecy. She believes you are the one to lead us. You will be the one to save our world that is under assault and will be actively more so soon. You are not some toy to be discarded when boredom overtakes. You are a strength we have waited for, will gather to, and will fight for and with, side by side."

We came to a tall wide door, "Walk into this room head held high and eyes wide open. See everything and miss nothing, be discreet, especially about your sister or you are doomed." He said and swung the door open silently on its great hinges.

I was dazed by what he said and felt like I was walking into a room full of predators. The chatter died and then stopped as I walked in the door. I appraised the room starting on the left and panning to the right, realizing I was dressed appropriately since everyone was dressed casually. I picked out a few who seemed too intent on what I would do; they reminded me of the great cats in the mountains who would stalk you looking for a weakness waiting for the kill. The cats had taught me to never show a weakness even if you didn't know what you were doing and to act like you are the biggest thing there.

My eyes swung back to Analise standing in the center of the group. Her idea of casual was a dress of gold ending just above the knee. It clung to her like a second skin and shimmered and flowed when she moved. I walked toward her noticing that the gold fire was brought out in her eyes by the dress. Green eyes dancing in gold, with flaming red hair cascading down her back, she was definitely the most beautiful woman here. As I approached she smiled that smile, I gave a short bow held out my hand and said, "My lady."

She nodded her head slightly as she took my hand, and asked, "Hungry?"

"I could eat a horse," I laughed.

"Great! That's what's on the menu." Then she laughed at my horrified look, "Just kidding, I was joking, we don't eat horses."

The tone was set for the evening, light and lively, and we headed for the tables.

"I knew you would be hungry so I ordered dinner to be served as soon as you arrived. We can talk and you can observe, then we will mingle after we have eaten." She said. "Everyone is most interested to meet you."

"I can tell, most of them have been looking hungrily at me. I thought maybe I was on the menu." I said.

"You noticed the predators?" She asked.

I grinned; we had the same thoughts about some of these people. Having the same ideas would help us work together, and hopefully keep surprises to a minimum.

We had the table at the head of the room of course, with views through the great windows to rival any anywhere. Majestic mountains covered in a snow that looked like cut diamonds, backed by a sky slowly darkening from a midnight blue to velvet black filling with its own version of diamonds. I was looking forward to seeing it in greater detail in the light of day. I don't remember what we ate but it was good and there was a lot of it. The beer and wine flowed freely and I would catch the words, blue eyes, now and again. Everyone seemed to be impressed with blue eyes; my eyes were the only blue eyes in the room, and as far as I knew the only ones in the kingdom, if this was a kingdom. I still hadn't figured that out regardless of what Dorian said.

Suddenly thoughts of my sister crashed into my brain. Were my blue eyes the only ones in this place? Where was my sister? Analise said she knew where she was and I glanced quickly around wondering if she was here in disguise with brown eyes. Those eyes I had seen belonged to my youngest sister, Violet; she's the one they hid. She's the one no one knew about. She would be fourteen now, what would she look like? Would she resemble mother or father? I had a sudden need to know where she was and that she was OK.

Analise felt the change in my mood and growing impatience with the meal and these people I did not know.

She leaned close and whispered, "What's wrong?"

"My sister," I replied, not bothering to whisper, "I need to see her. You know where she is, I must see her now."

"She is not here at the Castle. You must be patient and cautious, very few know of your sister and her real identity. Her safety relies on that continuing to be so. If certain people knew a member of your family survived besides you there would be real trouble and your lives depend on her anonymity, both of your lives until you are reunited" She said.

I looked at her and asked, "Why?"

"Because you have power, though you don't know its full potential yet and combined with your sister's power; Oh, yes she also has power; you have a great power no one can match. You have great need for revenge on those who destroyed your family, yet hers is greater. She has lived with it for twelve years and she knows they gave their lives so she would live. You slept for twelve years and just learned what happened. Your reunion is delicate and must be handled properly. You will not find a little girl who needs a protector."

Her words gave me a lot to think about and this was not the place to think. I remembered Dorian's advice to be discreet concerning Violet, I had said enough. I nodded my head once put my thoughts aside and gave my attention back to the room. No one had really paid attention to what we had talked about except one man who was tall and dark and reminded me of the man on the beach who swam away. I decided when the meal was over to make his acquaintance. If he was a friend he would be a good one to have, if he was an enemy, it would be good to know.

Chapter Eight

Analise and I was circling the room after dinner, she was introducing me to key people, though everyone seemed to want to meet me. Dorian never seemed far away from Analise and I found it comforting. I was filing away certain names to research and consider later. She was called away to tend to something and I turned to take a sweet from a tray carried by a servant and came face to face with the tall dark man. He managed a short bow with a smirk on his face.

"Georges La Roche," He said, "So you are the infamous blue eyes we have all been waiting for all these years. Did you have a good sleep? I am surprised you woke at all."

"Trevor Lee Dawson," I said, "I have never been one to sleep long." I took a step back to get a good look at this man, "I saw a man who sat on the beach, I sat a little way away and we watched a sunset together. He swam out into the ocean and did not come back."

"And I am interested in this little story for what reason?" He asked, staring intently at me.

"The man looked like you," I said. "He had just finished burying someone on the beach, and was watching the sunset. Having never seen the sun set over the ocean I also watched. After the green flash he swam away, giving me his coat and boots before he left. "

"Is that so," He asked, "Did this man say anything before he swam away? And was there anything in his pockets to identify him?"

I thought about that briefly then said, "He said he was passing through to another place. I didn't think to look in the pockets, but I will. You aren't a Silkie are you? I thought maybe he was a Silkie"

He looked at me with one eyebrow raised just as Analise breezed up with a big smile on her face.

"Georges, I see you have met Trevor." Looking at me she said, "I have some people I want you to meet."

Georges said, "Before you go, where did you see this man who looked like me?"

"A days trudge north of the Island landing, the last large grouping of rocks before the Rock Way. The grave is on the south side of the rocks. There is still a residue of a door I opened to escape thugs who wanted to bash my head in. It opened into the meadow below the castle so you should be able to find it."

His other eyebrow was now raised as he watched us leave. I was hoping he would seek me out when he returned, he didn't feel like an enemy. I knew he was going to check out what I had said; there was something else there in his eyes. I really wanted to get back to my room to check the pockets of the coat the man had given me. I was thinking about whether a Silkie needed a pelt or not to swim in the ocean when Analise started introducing me to a group of people. My mind was taken up by people with brown eyes and their astonishment at my own blue ones and I wondered just how rare are blue eyes especially if we are the only ones to be truly trusted?

I was finally in my room after meeting most of the people in the Great Room, they all had brown eyes. Most of them were surprised by my blue eyes; some even thought I had blue contacts which made me laugh. I was told most people had never seen a person with blue eyes. They thought they were a myth or extinct, and yet here I am.

Analise had said we would talk about my sister in the morning, it was late tonight and we were all tired. I was determined to hold her to that. I really needed to know where my sister was and what Analise meant when she said my sister wasn't helpless and that her feelings were different from mine. What had happened to my baby sister while I slept on the Island? I also still needed to find out who put me on that Island for 12 years. What exactly was that Island that I could sleep so long and live, and why did I wake up? A lot of people know about that island and seem surprised I woke up when I did. Was I supposed to sleep longer? All these thoughts went through my head as I searched for the coat the man on the beach had given me. I had expected it to be on the foot of the bed when I came back but it wasn't. I looked in closets and drawers, even the bathing chamber but could not locate it. I realized the boots were gone also since I had not seen them while I searched the room.

I sat down on the bed in frustration and noticed a small pile on the bedside table with a note. The note said my coat and boots had been taken to be cleaned and the pile was what was in the pockets. I looked up from the note and started sorting through the pile. There was a small rock that glittered, a small twisted piece of wood, a few copper pieces, a twisted piece of wire, a leather lace, a good knife that was sharp and a large silver piece with the head of a woman with curly hair on it.

I sat and looked at the pile that was now spread out on the table top. There was no paper or writing of any kind so I still had no idea who the man had been. I wondered if any of this stuff meant anything to anyone. I would just have to wait and see if anyone reacted to it, which meant I had to make it visible. I lay back on the bed and tried to think about that but my mind kept returning to my sister. I was getting nowhere with these thoughts so I went to bed and actually slept quite well. The last time I slept in a bed was home in the cabin. That was a few days ago to me and twelve years for everyone else. I was still surprised to wake up in one so big.

The next morning thoughts and memories rushed back into my head along with the promise Analise had given to talk about my sister. I got out of bed and opened the drapes to find the sun not yet peeking over the tops of the mountains and nothing had its sparkle yet. It was light enough that the stars were no longer visible. There was a knock on the door and I slipped into a pair of pants to answer it. Dorian stood there with my coat and boots in his hands frowning at me.

"You should put some clothes on to answer the door even if you make someone wait. You never know who is on the other side or what they might want. It could be your head they want for their mantle." He said.

Of course he was right and I told him so as I took my coat and boots from him, laying the coat on the bed. They looked like new and only now that the dirt was off could I admire the quality of the coat and boots the man from the beach had given me.

I looked at Dorian and asked, "Do you think I can find out who made this coat and these boots."

Dorian sighed, shook his head and said, "You are too trusting, what if I wanted to knock you over the head?"

"I would know," I said realizing I was right, I would know.

He stood and looked at me a minute then said, "Tailors usually mark their work on the inside of the garment. Same with the boots, though sometimes they mark the sole also with a sign of their trade." He picked up a boot to examine it as I went through the coat.

Nothing, everything had been torn out or scratched off; the man who swam away was not helping me a bit. I had no idea who he was but felt it was important that I know. Was there ever a chance meeting, others may think so but I did not, this man had something to tell me and he was going to make me work for it. Dorian looked at me with one eyebrow raised in question but I had no answers.

Chapter Nine

"Analise wishes to breakfast at sunrise and she requests your presence. I believe you two have a lot to discuss. There is a small breakfast room next to the kitchen with an east window to observe the rising sun, she should be there about now, you may want to get dressed and join her." He said; and handing me the boots he left.

I understood this to be Dorian's way of telling me to get my butt moving. I rinsed my hands in water and ran them over my face and through my hair then after a quick brush I tied it in its leather thong. I pulled on a shirt, this one a deep red, fleetingly wondering where they come from. I pulled on the soft boots for indoors and headed to the kitchen breakfast room after picking up my small pile of riff raff and stuffing it in my pockets. I remembered I did not show the pile of stuff to Dorian, and he may have recognized something. I will have to remember to show it to him later.

I entered the breakfast room and saw Analise gazing out the east window with a look of rapture on her face that was tinted a deep rose reflected from the rising sun. I stood behind her and watched as the sun tipped over the tallest mountain, and turned the world from rose colored to a wonderland of sparkling diamonds as the light slid down the slope and crawled toward the castle. Analise's face was filled with rapture and she joyously clapped her hands and laughed a light carefree laugh I had not heard. This was way more then observing for her, it felt like a ritual that allowed her to just be herself for a little while.

I moved around from behind her and sat so I could see out the window at the sun drenched mountains, or look at her face. At this moment with the joy of the new sun shining on her, she was truly a beautiful woman. It was something I had started to notice and it was rammed home in my gut at this moment and I lifted my hand to brush a stray strand of hair like fire back from her face. The moment passed as the sun took its rightful place in the sky; she looked at me with a sober face, and was back to business as usual.

She spoke, "Your youngest sister Violet was hidden when the attack on your home was eminent. Your family knew it was coming and prepared a place for her to be safe. Since she was born at home and they had had minimum contact outside the mountains no one knew about her and your family knew there was a good chance she would escape. A signal was devised to alert Friends who went to aid them as soon as it was received and they hoped to arrive in time to help. Your father, mother and other three sisters all knew they were going to die, even the youngest."

"Those who sent the murderers," she continued, "for that is what they are, were determined to wipe blue eyes from the face of the earth. Your family fought well and few of the attackers left the field of battle. Those who left knew they could not call it a victory when so many had died trying to kill children who out fought them until they died among the many enemies they dropped at their feet. They did not even take their dead there were so few left alive and so many dead. When the Friends reached your home in the mountains all they found were dead and one little girl curled up in a nest with her favorite doll, her thumb in her mouth and tears dried on her face. It seems your family has a strong connection and little Violet had seen the entire battle through your family's eyes even though they tried to shield her. She knew they were dead and insisted on lighting the funeral pyre from a torch her little hands could hold. Violet spat on the murderers being picked over by the crows and said, "Let them rot," in her little girl voice."

"The Friends were amazed by the fierceness in this child. They chose to honor your fathers request and channel that fierceness into a tool that could be used, a tool to bring down those who want to bring chaos back into the world. Essentially those who destroyed your family did it because blue eyes stand for the truth and with truth chaos cannot reign. Your father had requested Violet be taken to the Palace of the Assassins; in fact she begged to be taken to the Palace. She insisted her father had told her she must be ready when her brother returns because the two of you would turn the world to fire."

She leaned back in her chair and sighed through lips in a pale face and said, "Now you know where your sister has been for the last twelve years and believe me she is ready to kick some nasty ass."

The vulgar word from her mouth brought me back to myself. I shook my head as if to clear it knowing nothing was going to clear this up except death, and a lot of it. Revenge is a dish best served cold; well I was in a cold country lets get to it. There was a flash in the meadow in front of the castle, Georges was on his way, it had begun. I didn't know what, but I knew it had begun.

"I need to go to the Palace of the Assassins," I said.

Analise raised her hand and said, "Breakfast first."

Servers came in with trays of food that smelled like heaven on earth and looked even better, and who can pass up heaven first thing in the morning. I found myself ravenous after Analise's dialog and she ate heartily also, it was as if we both knew this was a new beginning and we needed to be well fortified for what was to come.

The Palace of Assassins was far from the castle over several mountain passes. Analise could not project a picture of the palace since she had never been there but I knew I could open a door to it if I could see it. I could not simply access her memories, she had learned quickly from me how to raise a door. I now had to knock at a golden door carved with trees, flowers and birds to talk to her. I had not seen the door in the castle and wondered where the original was. She told me Dorian had been there and I could possibly get a vision from him so she sent a servant to ask him to come to the breakfast room. We watched the wind outside the window playing with snow snakes that glittered like diamonds while we waited.

Dorian arrived shortly and was not sure he wanted me playing around in his head when I explained what I wanted.

"You only need to project the vision of the palace into the front of your mind and concentrate on that letting it fill up your mind and that will be the only thing I see." I told him. "I give you my word I will not look further."

He looked into my eyes and slowly nodded his head. He sat across from me and leaned back in the chair, brow furrowing as he concentrated. I looked into his mind and saw a large Palace of white that seemed made of ice with twelve turrets. It sat on the highest peak of the surrounding mountains, and looked like it floated in the clouds it was so high. It glimmered and shifted, one moment it looked like it wasn't there then it was back. Most people would never even see it. On a plateau about half way up the mountain was the beginning of a stair that was black as death and clear of snow, it wound around and up to the entrance of the Place of Assassins. As I was pulling myself from Dorian's mind a large dark and menacing presence made itself known, pressing around the edges of the vision as if it wanted to suck me in. I sat back accessing what I had seen.

Dorian asked, "What did you see?"

I related what I saw leaving out the darkness at the end. My respect for him had grown; keeping such a powerful psyche in control required a great will.

"You have a gentle touch," he said, "you will only be able to open a door at the bottom of the stair. The magic qualities that keep the Palace hidden will not allow a door any closer."

"I seem to be able to do things I have never done before, it's like I woke up with these abilities and new ones keep cropping up. You have had this done before?" I said.

"Of course, you don't live as long as I have lived and not had your mind probed by blue eyes. Your father had a gentle touch also, and your mothers touch was like a caress." He said.

"You knew my parents?" I asked.

"Who do you think took Violet to the Palace? I would let no one else touch that child. She was to be protected at all cost. Your family paid dearly to keep her safe and I lost good friends that day. I will go with you to the Palace to see Violet. She has much to tell you that will be a surprise and a shock." He said, and then would say no more.

I was already a bit shocked, how did I not know this man or remember him from somewhere if my parents were his friends.

"I do not understand how this could be so." I said.

"You were a child when events overtook your family. You still believed the world revolved around you. Children do not see, nor are shown everything. You will understand more in time and that is as it should be." He replied, and then turned to Analise. "We will need to travel light, with two others as look outs besides us three. Five will not be deemed a threat. I will go and make arrangements, arriving just before dinner will be a good time, meet me in the great room just before dark. They can offer hospitality, and there will be no awkwardness if we break bread with them, there is also less of a chance of getting our throats slit. They frown on killing those they have fed, though it has been done." He rose to go and we both just nodded our heads in agreement in a kind of stunned silence.

We looked at each other and I asked, "Did you expect to go?"

"I really wanted to and thought I would have to argue with Dorian to get him to see my point. I was even ready to pull rank to go, I guess he knew that." She said. "Well, we had better get ready if we are going to be there this afternoon."

We parted ways to prepare for our journey. I went back to my room remembering I had not shown the riff raff in my pocket to either Analise or Dorian. Interesting, I wondered why I would forget, it was as if something in my pocket didn't want to be seen. I pulled it out and laid everything on my dresser, I looked at it for a moment then picked up my pack and started packing. I took everything I had brought and most of my new clothes. I believe in being prepared. We planned on being back tomorrow or the next day at latest but things change and if you are in the field and are not prepared when things change then you live with what you have.

Chapter Ten

My coat was laid out and I was pulling on my boots when there was a knock on my door. I pulled on my boots then went to answer the door. Alert and ready enough to please Dorian I opened the door a crack and peered out to see Georges standing there with a hang dog face. Shit, now what? I thought. I opened the door enough to let him in and guided him to a chair.

"What is it?" I asked, "You look like you have seen death."

"I have, Trevor I have." He said. "Death of hope, death of life, and death of a niece I never knew. Death of my brother, the other half of my soul, my twin, I went where the man on the beach was and this is what I found. If only he would have sought me out I could have helped him or at least been there for him. I have searched for him for many years, and you find him sitting on a beach. And no he or we are not Silkies, if he swam into the ocean the way you described he swam to his death. But there is no body and if there is no body anything is possible. That is the only hope I have."

I got up and scooped up the riff raff from my dresser and laid it out on the low table in front of him. I heard his gasp as he reached for the silver piece with the woman with the curly hair.

He cupped it in his hand then laid it against his cheek rubbing it like a cat.

"We were given identical coins when we were twelve by our grandmother. She said whoever still had the coin when we turned twenty would inherit the bulk of her estate." He reached into his pocket and pulled out an identical coin. Cradling them one in each hand, he laughed, and said, "A cousin inherited, neither I nor Jonas could part with our coin. I have never seen it out of his presence until now. If you do not mind I would have the two reunited until I find my brother or his body."

I told him the coin had waited for him and was his for as long as it is meant to be. I scooped up the rest of the stuff and dropped it into a bag handing that to him also. I told him he may find something of interest in the rest of the stuff from his brother's pockets. If he did not mind I would like to keep the coat and boots. He took the bag and said the coat and boots was a gift from his brother and he could never take it from me. Wear it in good health were his sentiments. He turned to leave and turned back holding out his hand, he shook my hand with tears in his eyes.

"I thank you, Trevor. It has been many years since I even knew where my brother was. We chose different paths and I feared he was lost. Then he completely disappeared. I appreciate the chance to find him again even if it's to see his dead body. I had the girl child disinterred and moved to our family cemetery." He said, his voice shaking. "If I can ever assist you in any way please seek me out."

After he left I slowly finished packing thinking about what had just transpired. I knew how it felt to lose family; I had not yet grieved for those who died. Grieving would have to wait until I could visit the site of our mountain home after I have killed those responsible. Georges was in limbo until he could find or come to terms with the loss of his brother. I felt sorrow for the man I just met and the man who swam away. I put these thoughts away; I had to find my sister and shouldering my pack headed to the great room.

Everyone thought the same way I did and had well packed packs. I swung mine off my shoulder and set it on the floor. Analise was dressed in black leather pants and a green silk shirt that shimmered and sturdy leather boots. She wore a long leather coat that shone like gold with a golden fur ruff around the hood. Her pack was not as large as mine but well heeled. I checked out the others and they all had sturdy well used equipment. I could tell by what they wore they were all used to living in the conditions we were going to.

"This is John and Owen, our lookouts," He said, then

Dorian asked, "Can you open a door from here or do we need to go outside?"

"Why can't you open a door?" I asked and for a second thought he was going to hit me. I watched him visibly calm himself down and said, "I meant no offence, Dorian, I just don't know why I can and you can't."

"It is an innate ability, you have to be born with it and not a lot of people are." He replied.

"I seem to be able to recognize it in other people; I knew Georges could open a door and told him where to find his brother. It's sameness, recognizing a like soul. My father could not open a door could he?" I asked.

"If he could have your family would be here today, now we must go and see the family you have left to you." He said.

"It would be better to open a door outside. A door leaves a trail that someone could follow back. It would be better if they had to knock instead of just showing up inside the castle." I said. Dorian looked at me, surprised I would think of that, I was a little surprised myself.

We all picked up our gear and trooped outside into the courtyard then through the gate into the meadow where I had arrived. They started to put down their gear when a door slid into existence. We looked through into a deep valley full of sparkling snow and a black stair rising from the plateau and spiraling up into the clouds. I stepped through and the rest followed. As the last person stepped through, the door winked out. We started walking through the snow toward the stairs. There was a hard crust to walk on so we did not sink in and made good time. We arrived at the base of the stairs, they were six feet wide and eighteen inches deep made of some kind of black stone that felt warm to the touch. It curved unbroken up the mountain and into the clouds. I could feel the magic humming through the stone. There was a sign carved into stone next to the first step

and we all read;

10,000 Steps into the Clouds,
10,000 Sighs,
10,000 cries,
10,000 Ways to Die.

"They don't make it very inviting do they? I said.

"They are not the type to invite." Dorian replied. "Many people have died on these steps, so step lively and do not stop. The stairs have a way of changing if you stop and you may not like what it does.

"We cannot stop and rest?" Analise gasped, "We walk up 10,000 steps and not stop?"

"That's right; Trevor's sister did it at age three. Everyone walks these steps, and no one stops, if you want to go to the Palace of Assassin."

I was beginning to wonder if I had over packed but everyone else had about the same size pack I did, so there must be a reason for what we carry. I hoisted my pack and walked in a circle testing it and decided I could carry it. I had been thinking and yes Violet had had a birthday between the time I left and my family was killed. That would make her fourteen almost fifteen.

"Well then, lets get started it's not going to get any earlier or easier if we stand around." I said.

I put my foot upon the first stair and it was like I was compelled to take the next step. Analise was behind me, then Dorian, John and Owen brought up the rear walking together. It was this way we walked the 10,000 steps. We could not pass each other and none of us slowed down. We did not look over the edge or up or down. We kept a steady pace and when our legs started to burn no one complained, when they started to cramp we did not stop. By the time we reached the top and our legs felt like dead sticks of wood we would not even consider sitting down because they might break in half and we would never get up. We finally stood at the top of the stair before the entrance to the palace. We actually stopped because we had to ring a bell then wait for it to be answered. We swayed slightly and felt a tingling begin in our legs from inactivity after our climb. There was the possibility our legs might still be alive as the tingling began to turn into a steady burn. I looked at the palace and it did not disappear like it did from afar but I could understand how it would look like it did. It was white, blindingly white and it glowed as if it had a life of its own and did not want just anyone to see it. The lintel as well as the door itself was plain and the plainness made it beautiful. The door finally swung in and a tall figure stood before us. He was dressed in white leggings; pants, tunic, and a long over coat with its hood were all a pure white. The face that peered out at us was black and looked familiar. He gestured us in with a black hand and as Dorian passed the hand rested lightly on his shoulder and the word, brother, was uttered. It clicked why he looked familiar and why Dorian knew so much about the Palace of the Assassins.

CHAPTER ELEVEN

Once inside we were greeted by three more persons in white, two men and one woman.

"Welcome Trevor, and your companions. We have waited long for this joining. You must come, rest, eat and drink with us. We have much to talk about after a proper time has passed." The woman said.

"I thank you madam, for your offer of hospitality. It is much appreciated as well as needed." I replied as my legs began to shake involuntarily and another step seemed impossible.

She led us into a room where we could refresh ourselves and had drink brought to us.

"Drink deeply and waste nothing and you will feel like new shortly." She advised.

Analise sniffed but took her advise and the rest of us did as well, we were all shaking uncontrollably. In no time after drinking the drought she had brought we were completely refreshed and feeling like we could climb those 10,000 steps again. We were shown places to stow our packs. Then we were led to a dinning hall where long tables were set up and being filled with delicious food. There was a huge variety that smelled like heaven and con-sidering how close we were it could be heaven we were so hungry. We were shown to a table by Dorian's brother and told where to sit then he left us. We sat and we waited.

Soon the tables were filled and people in white started to file in, all humming some strange tune and carrying bowls and spoons. Five of the people who sat at our table handed each of us a bowl and spoon. They all stood and when I started to stand Dorian pulled me back down. They all suddenly stomped one foot and sat. We ate in silence; all we could eat was put away with a determination that there may not be another meal, ever. The food was gone and just as suddenly the tables were clear. I looked around wondering what next when I heard my name.

"Trevor lee Dawson, what is it you seek?" a soft voice said. It was repeated over and over louder each time.

Analise looked at me with a worried expression on her face. I stood and faced the room full of assassins and the question died.

"I seek my sister who came here when she was three, Violet Marie Dawson." I said.

"Vi, Vi, Violet, Violet Marie Dawson what say you?" the voices asked.

"Why, why, why, why?" the voices repeated.

I think about this question, indeed why? She was a baby when I left. What connection do we have anymore? Blood, we have blood. What else is there? And so I answer.

"Blood, we have the same blood. We are connected across the years and for all time. We are the only two left in this world who carry our blood. Family, I want my family back and she is all that is left. I need her, probably more then she needs me. But I need my sister." I said.

Slowly a tall lithe figure stands up on the far side of the room and comes around the tables heading for me. This figure moves with a lions grace and a sureness that's puts us all to shame. Stopping in front of me the hood is thrown back and a pair of huge blue eyes stares at me at eye level. The red gold hair is cropped short and sticks up all around her head. Her face is sculpted just like our mothers and she is beautiful. It's the first thing out of my mouth.

"God, you look like mother, you grew up beautiful Violet." I said.

"I grew up more then that." She replied.

The next thing I knew I was flat on my back and she was straddling me and chiding me, "Brother, surely you can do better then that."

I saw Analise start to get up and Dorian pull her down. Shit, this was deep I thought, I see my little sister for the first time in twelve years and she tries to kill me so much for hugs. I reached up grabbed my baby sisters hair and with a knee jerk threw her over my head where she rolled and bounded to her feet already heading back toward me. I spun on my shoulders and kicked her feet out from under her. She came down on her side and spun to put a kick to my head. I grabbed her foot and twisted shoving at the same time. She slid across the floor and I had time to get to my feet. She bounced to her feet and we faced each other.

"Pissed off I slept for twelve years while you got to grow up in Assassin land?" I asked.

"Did you? Did you sleep for twelve years?" she asked.

"What do you mean by that?" I snarled.

"I mean you reacted pretty fast for someone who did not grow up in Assassin land. How did you learn those moves sleeping all those years?" She chided again.

She had a point I thought, how do I know to move and do the things I do? Like open doors to other places. I had been taking them for granted that I just knew, part of growing up and all that. Problem was I didn't grow up. I felt a knife flying through and parting the air toward my head from my sister's hand. I turned my head and I could see the trail the knife left in the air. I held up my hands and the knife slowed as it sped toward my head. It hovered between my hands, and then I plucked it out of the air and tossed it up and down.

"What do you know I don't know?" I asked.

"I know the more you are exposed to the more you wake. That the more you need the more you can do that seems impossible to the rest of us. I know that father wove a spell in that bag you slept in for twelve years before he put you on that island. I was there. I know you truly did not sleep, but you learned things the rest of us will never know as long as we live. You can do things we have never seen. You will lead us on great paths and cleanse us of all the evils that chew us to death. I know that you are a great man. I know you are my brother and I will follow you to the end of the earth and do all I can to protect the dream of the reality we will live one day because of you." She said all of this as she walked toward me. She knelt at my feet and bowed her head.

"I will never lift a hand toward you again as long as I live," she said, then looking up she smiled, "Unless of course, you need some sense knocked into your thick head, my brother."

I was stunned by what she said. My father had put me on that island, and had put a spell on me? That is when I noticed the silence. I glanced around and everyone was looking at us as stunned as I felt. I looked down into Violets blue eyes so like my own and she laughed. I smiled, reached down and pulled her to her feet and we both laughed. We threw back our heads and peels of laughter rang from us and tears ran down our faces as we hugged each other. I finally led my little sister back to our table and introduced her to Analise and the others. Analise cautiously held her hand out in greeting, Violet assured her she would not bite, just yet. The rumble of after dinner conversations had resumed all around us as we sat.

"We need to talk," I told Violet, as I picked up a beer.

"We will have plenty of time," she said, "I plan on coming with you where ever you are going. I am ready to leave this place; it has taught me all I need to know."

"Are you considered an Assassin then?" Analise asked. "I heard you can leave only when all the training is complete."

"That remains to be seen," Violet replied, "It depends on what my brother needs done, or I deem necessary for his and thus the worlds greater good." She cocked her head, and then said, "I remember you, at the castle on the way to the palace. You were the young princess Dorian was so fond of. You were also the voice in my brother's head. Are you proud of what you did?"

Analise's face went white, "I did nothing except call for help and a young man answered me in my darkness. I was devastated when he was lost to me, and overjoyed when he returned. I do not know what else you could be referring to." She said.

"Let's hope you speak truth, my brother seems fond of you." Violet replied.

At that Analise's face turned red but she held her tongue. The man who had led us here approached and said sleeping rooms had been made ready for us and if we would follow he would show us to them. Dorian walked next to him as we followed and they murmured together in low voices. When we reached our rooms Violet put a hand on my arm holding me back.

"I must leave you now," she said, "When you go into your room shut the door and lock it. Do not come out. Let no one in until I come in the morning. No one, understand?"

❧

CHAPTER TWELVE

Strangely enough I did understand. Violet turned and left, walking with the grace of a lioness few could copy. I was shown to my room by who I was positive by now was Dorian's brother. I told everyone good night and entered a small and barren room. There was a bed in one corner and no lock on the door. I laughed, then concentrated and locked the door. As tired as I suddenly was, I decided to soundproof it also and fell into a deep uninterrupted sleep. That's why I did not hear all the commotion in the night. I came out of my room when Violet knocked inside my head the next morning, refreshed and ready for the day. Everyone else in my party was tired, ragged and worn out. It seems someone tried to break into my room and when that didn't work broke into Analise's room thinking I would come rushing out to save her. The rest of our party rushed to her defense and were able to beat off the attackers. Of course I heard none of it, sleeping soundly through it all. I made a note to myself to from now on lock Analise's room also and maybe soundproofing was not a good idea. I asked Analise if she was alright and she nodded. Violet stood back and observed it all. It was hard to remember this strong lithe, composed young woman was my baby sister of fourteen. I truly believed she could kill everyone in the room and I was probably not wrong. I could see in her eyes she was furious, who in the Palace would dare hurt her brother or anyone connected to him. Twelve years in the Palace of Assassins had made her lethal; they had known better then to go after Violet, because they would now be dead.

Violet looked at me with one eyebrow raised. Hmmm, I wonder how much of my thoughts she can hear. She raised the other eyebrow. OK, we need to talk and sooner the better. I had no idea what is going on. My dad may have woven a teaching spell into my sleeping bag but he left out a lot of information I needed, like what the hell is going on in the world.

I looked at my weary group of travelers plus my sister and said, "We need to go back to Castle Clarion, and I need some answers, so I can decide what to do and where we need to be next. I may have as Violet said learned a great deal in the twelve years I slept, but I still slept. I have no idea what is going on in the world or why it needs someone like me."

They all looked at me nodded their heads and we headed for breakfast. We all needed to eat and I hoped it would refresh those who had not slept much last night. We all searched the faces in the dining room and saw nothing that gave us a clue as to who or why we were attacked last night. I wondered as we finished eating if anything would be done about it, an investigation of sorts.

"Trevor Lee Dawson, you are summoned before the Council of Assassins." Resounded throughout the hall and two people dressed in white appeared behind my seat. I looked around at my friends then rose to be escorted to the Council. Their eyes followed me as I walked away but even my sister did not rise to follow me.

We walked along corridors and turned corners until I was dizzy but I knew I was not lost. I could unerringly return to the dining hall, I could feel my way back and was comforted by that feeling. We finally stood before a great black door, again unmarked. My escorts stepped back and stood on either side of the door and I knew I should proceed alone.

I pushed gently at that great black door and it silently swung in to reveal a large circular room with walls filled with books from top to bottom. There was a tall ladder on a track that could be pushed around to reach books on high shelves. The domed ceiling had a circular skylight that lit the room with a strong but soft light that revealed paintings on the ceiling and walls wherever there were not books. There were groupings of leather chairs and small wooden tables around the perimeter. A large round table made of black marble was in the center directly under the skylight. The three people who had greeted us when we arrived stood on the other side of that table. Above the table rotated a sword so black it seemed to absorb all the light around it then send it back into the atmosphere from its tip charged with energy. I slowly advanced into the room and up to the table never taking my eyes off the sword.

I stopped when I bumped into the table; I had been so entranced by the sword. I glanced at the three assassins then looked back at the sword. Its turning captured me once again then the point settled steady in the air pointing directly at my heart.

The sword spoke to me in my head ["You are mine; we have been joined at your birth and will only part at your death, which will never happen with me at your side."] A bolt of energy shot out of its tip and I felt a searing pain above my heart, then cold. My mind opened to a great light and information poured in. Evil that wished to control the world focused on a large black shadow. There were great black beasts that roamed the world and were ripping and gouging the earth and its people as they stood helpless. There were beings that were vaguely human turning man against man. And evil men were choosing to follow the black shadow, where I could just make out the shape of a man with a stick in one hand, whip in the other and a black brimmed hat pulled low. Blazing red eyes peered out from under that brim and right into mine; The Dark Man. The skies boiled and the earth heaved. The mountains fell and the oceans rose commanded by the darkness, washing away all that was ever good in this world and remaking it in its image.

A voice spoke out loud and brought me back to this room I stood in. I was now holding the sword in my right hand, my shirt was ripped open and a glowing black mark in the shape of the sword I held was centered above my heart.

"This is what you must stop, you who are the one, the wielder the Black Sword. It is only you who can halt the march of darkness across this world and the rending of its very fabric so no man or woman survives. You are the one who will excise the evil and heal the world through blood and fire setting the Dark Man in his place. You were born thus, you were trained for this, and you are the hope of the world." The woman in white who stood in the center said.

I took my gaze off the sword and looked at the three across the now seeming empty table. I nodded my head, touched the sword to my forehead saluting them then sheathed it in the scabbard that had appeared on my side. I turned and strode from the room and down the corridor not waiting for my guides. I now knew what I fought and why. I was determined to stop this evil, the evil that destroyed my family and threatened to destroy the entire world. Not on my watch it wouldn't I thought as I strode into the dining hall and standing at the head of the room I drew the black sword and held it high. The words, "Black Sword, flew around the room in hushed whispers, then again louder.

"The world is being torn asunder by an evil so great it will claim many of you. I tell you this, darkness will not have victory. It will fall before the light and die never to rise again. I will be there to stomp it into oblivion and any who join the dark." I said. My sword lowered as five men rose starting toward me with death in their eyes, lightening shot from its end and they died where they had stood, vaporized into nothingness. Others stood in surprise and shock.

"I will call on all of you and you will come to the aid of the world or die with the darkness, because the darkness will die." I sheathed my sword and strode to my companions. "It is time to leave." I said to the faces of my friends with their rounded eyes and dropped jaws.

CHAPTER THIRTEEN

Analise stared at my torn shirt and what was underneath, and then without a blink rose to go. My sister had been the first up and the only one who did not seem surprised, we need to have that talk I thought. John and Owen took a step back as if they were afraid of me then stiffened their backs and stood where they were. Dorian did not move, I could see the gears turning in his head as he assimilated then accepted this turn of events. Our gear was delivered to us, we shouldered our packs and as we left every knee in that great hall bent at our passing. Most of them rose and followed us out the great doors. I gazed out at the valley far below and the great black stair that rose from below. I knew this would be the last moment of peace we would enjoy for a long while. I drew the black sword and opened a door at the top of the steps to every ones surprise. The door opened into the meadow before the Castle Clarion and madness beyond. The enemy had broached us on our own ground. I let out a fierce yell and heard steal ringing in my ears as hundreds of swords were drawn at my back and we leapt through the door and into the battle, and the blood already soaking into the field.

Violet was at my back and hacking into the fray as we worked our way toward the gates of the castle. She fought like a ballet dancer bringing to it a bloody beauty as she danced the dance of death she had learned so well. I felt the door from the Palace click shut as the last Assassin leapt through. The Black Sword cut a swath through the enemy with bolts of energy like lightning as we slowly moved forward. The gates had not been breached yet and I thought of the women and children inside. I knew they would all be armed but I did not want the enemy inside the castle, it was our only strong hold. Analise was fighting beside us with Dorian at her back and I could knew we all had the same goal. Hold the gates of Castle Clarion and destroy this enemy.

It had started to snow and darkness was descending as the sun slowly sank into the mountains in this part of the world. Huge black beasts rushed out of the darkness to gouge out our flanks. As we came closer to the gates archers on the wall started shooting burning arrows into the sides of the beasts and they flared and burned as if they were made of oil. The burning beasts gave us light to continue the fight that lasted long into the night. We lost people but the enemy lost many more trying to overwhelm us with numbers instead of skill. Skill will win every time and soon it was a rout. They ran into the dark sloshing through the blood of their comrades with shrieking howls. We stood and watched them go leaning on our weapons with the stench of the burning beasts in our nostrils and our own share of blood to trek through. The gates had not been breached.

Georges La Roche trudged up to us standing before the gates. He was favoring his left arm that was wrapped with a rag torn from his shirt. He said, "You arrived just in time Trevor; I thought we had lost the day overwhelmed by shear numbers when you came charging out of that door. Whoever you brought with you definitely turned the tide. They sure knew how to fight, where did they all come from?"

I lifted the Black Sword so he could see it and said, "I emptied the Palace of the Assassins."

"The Black Sword," His face paled when he saw the sword burned into my skin over my heart and he said, "So the legend is true and you are that Blue Eyes?"

I sighed and said, "It seems that it is so." I turned to my sister. "Violet, meet Georges La Roche, Georges my sister Violet."

Georges stared at Violet and she gazed back at him.

"Yes," he said, "We have met in my dreams."

"Mine as well," Violet said.

I looked at one then the other and sighed again, "Of course." I said.

Analise turned to me and said, "The gates must be opened and the people gotten inside. There are those that are injured and must be tended and we must take note of those who have fallen and notify their families. Then we must prepare a funeral pyre for them out from the east door. Their names will be inscribed upon the walls for all to remember."

We all turned to the gates as they swung open and the people from inside poured out to help us get the injured and the fallen inside. The battle was over but the night was not, we had much to do though we had lost fewer people then expected and none of the assassins. We made large piles of the enemy dead far from the castle and had the archers set them afire. The black smoke boiled into the air but it was far enough away we were not bothered by the stench. The injured were housed on pallets in the great hall to make it easier to care for them. The doctor was making his rounds marking those in need of the most urgent care. Analise had disappeared seeking the families of those who had fallen in battle to inform them of their loss and give what comfort she could. The sun had been well up before we had the chance to rest. We had grabbed food and drink on the move in the night so the biggest necessity we needed was rest. Tired people make mistakes. I stood on the wall gazing over the meadow; there was nothing we could do about the blood saturating the snow. Hopefully the next storm will blot it out and we can move on though never forget what is under our feet. The smoke from the burning enemy dead was diminishing and at sunset we would take our dead out the Postern gate. It would be as far away as we could take them from these fires and the blood soaked meadow for their own funeral.

I went back into the castle; I heard voices from the breakfast room but passed it on by. I was weary, filthy and no fit company for anyone. I stumbled to my room and smelled the sweet sent of a bath. I laid the Black Sword on the bed in its scabbard; I needed to clean it later. I dropped my clothes along the way to the bath and sank into and under the hot water. I came up for breath and scrubbed until my skin was red and the sent of blood and smoke was gone from my hair and body. I climbed out of the tub in a daze and wrapped up in a fluffy towel, how did they do that? I made it to my bed noticing my dirty clothes were gone on the way, but the sword lay where I left it. I fell into bed and was asleep before my head hit the pillow. Then someone was banging on my door. Groggily I fell off the bed and remembered to grab the towel on the way to the door. I opened it and Dorian stood there with my clothes cleaned and pressed, how did they do that?

Dorian said, "You should answer your door dressed, someone could want to take off your head, but then you would probably know that."

I nodded and said, "I was sleeping. This is becoming a habit, you bringing me my clean clothes."

He tipped his head gazing at the sword burned into my flesh and said, "It is time to honor our dead, the sun sets."

I nodded and took my clothes. He bent over and handed me my cleaned boots and my pack. I don't even know where I had dropped it but was glad to have it back.

"I will wait here." He said, closing the door.

I splashed water on my face, combed and tied back my hair and quickly got dressed. I buckled on the scabbard of the Black Sword realizing as I did that it was clean. Who, I wondered would dare touch it, realizing no one would. The Black Sword had cleaned itself, I was not really surprised but I had to think about it later. I shrugged into my coat and opened the door. Dorian hand-ed me a cup of hot liquid that went a long way toward restoring me, I wondered if it was like what we had in the Palace of the Assassins. We stepped into the end of the line filing out the Postern Gate. There were four assassins to each liter carrying a dead comrade. They were showing their respect for those fallen in battle by carrying them to their final rest. There were twelve in all and twelve pyres to place them upon arranged in a circle.

Chapter Fourteen

Everyone circled the twelve pyres but I continued into the center of the circle. The bodies wrapped in their shrouds were laid upon the wood as their families wept their farewells. The wood was lit and the fires flared red then blue as they climbed into the sky. I unsheathed the Black Sword and everyone looked at me even those who were bowed in sorrow. I raised the Black Sword high over my head pointed to the stars.

"To those fallen in battle I give you your victory song." I said and bringing it down I touched the Sword to my forehead and it sang. I could feel the sword burned into my chest get warm and get hotter with each note. Raising the Sword again to the stars it soared and cried, it triumphed, it bellowed, it lowed sweet and strong resounding off the surrounding mountains. The song wrenched every heart and soul that stood listening to its song. It sang as the flames danced and the billowing smoke ascended escorting the souls of the dead into the stars. Everyone was swaying on their feet to the song the sword sang. In one final sweet note the Black Sword fell silent and in a final tribute to our dead lightning shot from its tip and into the heavens lighting the sky in its brilliance. I then pointed the sword at the castle wall and the names of the dead were written in fire upon the wall to join those of their ancestors. The crowd stepped back and then roared in appreciation of what the sword had written. I sheathed the sword and walked out of the circle toward the gate, the people parted to let me pass some falling upon their knees. Dorian fell in walking beside me with Analise on the other side, Georges and Violet behind me. Everyone followed in silence until we were all back inside and the gate was shut against our enemies.

The Assassins needed to go back to the Palace. In the Great Hall I opened a door to the top of the stairs of the Palace of Assassins. The injured and those attending them cheered as they filed through. The last assassin was Dorian's brother and he paused at the door.

"My name is Gabriel; we will come when we hear the sword sing in battle. You and your people will not fight the darkness alone, Trevor." He said, and touching his forehead in salute he stepped through the door and was gone. I closed the door upon the cold high night.

Our small group gathered in the breakfast room and over coffee, tea and left over breakfast rolls and slices of meat we discussed what had happened and what was coming. Georges told us the enemy and their beasts came through a door and attacked a hunting party returning to the castle. An alarm was given and men from the castle rushed to their aid and the battle was on. It had been raging back and forth for about an hour and a half when our door had opened and we charged in. If we had not come at that time the people and castle would have been overrun by shear numbers. The enemy simply stepped over their dead and continued to fight.

I told them what I had learned in the Council of the Assassins about the dark man with the blazing eyes who wanted to rule the world. Not the good world but to turn everything black and evil. He wanted to make the daylight dark and the night's blacker killing anything that stood for light, peace and goodness. He carried a stick that I was sure had some sort of magic in it. He used his black beasts to scare and intimidate and his evil men to kill maim and herd the people who wanted only good in their lives. If he could not turn them he used drugs or simply killed them, entire families and entire villages were wiped out in his wake. When I finished I looked around at faces that had gone pale at the thought of what was to come.

Georges said, "So what we fought was a small battle in the war to come and if we don't win horrors will be visited upon our world we can't even imagine. Otherwise the worst of the worst is what we have to expect."

I nodded my head and looking at each of them, I said, "We will win this war and send the dark man to hell where he belongs. If he wants darkness and evil let him find it there. Our world belongs to the light and it will remain in the light. We must send outriders to track the beasts that were here and find out if they returned through a door. We must send emissaries to the other Kingdoms and to all people who stand for good telling them to prepare. They must make weapons and gather, ready for a great war. This is not a war for dominance; it is a war we fight for our right to live in the light and we must be bound together."

Dorian said, "I will send riders to track the beasts with the dawn. They will find evidence of a door or the bests themselves. They can't have gone far in these mountains. It would be good to capture a couple to question."

Analise said, "We should send men in groups of three dressed in Clarion livery and wearing the Crest of Clarion upon their breasts as emissaries to the other Kingdoms. That way people will know they speak truth with us at their backs."

I agreed and said, "Dorian it would be good if we could have someone to question if they didn't slip through a door." Turning to Analise I said, "Choose your men; we should have at least five groups. I will send them through doors to their destinations and will stand by to bring them back. We cannot leave them anywhere long since we do not know where the dark man has infiltrated. Tell them to be on high alert, prepared for anything. They must reach those in charge quickly, deliver the message and return."

Georges said, "I will work out what they are to say to get the urgency across clearly and quickly."

"I will be sure they are armed for the greatest affect and personal protection." Violet volunteered.

We all rose and went our separate ways with the plan to meet in the great room in an hour.

Dorian had his outriders prepared and ready to ride at the dawn. Analise had her fifteen men chosen and dressed in Clarion livery. Violet had taken them to the armory and they were armed to the teeth with throwing stars under their belts, knives in their boots and rapiers in a scabbard down the inside of the backs of their coats. I'm sure they had a few more surprises on them as well as their visible weapons and I gave a nod to Violet. She took her work seriously. Georges had come in with a short message honed to the point we wanted to make and was having all fifteen men memorize it. The message included that the Black Sword was in the world to fight for good once again.

At the end of the Great Room away from the injured I prepared to open five doors. We were targeting the closest Kingdoms first and I knew I could open a door right into their Great Rooms I could also leave no trace of the door for someone to follow back. Analise had chosen John to stand by a door while she, Violet, Dorian, and Georges stood by the others. I would oversee them all and pull the men out and close the door quickly if necessary. The men in groups of three were standing ready to enter the doors. They were instructed to stand back to back in a circle the one facing the King was to speak with all respect and to be prepared for anything. Answer questions but be quick and instill urgency. I opened the doors into castles Teague, Peloria, Reston, Solaria, and Minorca. The men stepped forward and into the Great Rooms of the castles. We could hear surprised outcries then murmurs and questions after the message was delivered. All five groups were back with us in a short time and all reported favorably that each castle was preparing for war as we spoke. We repeated opening doors at the next five closest castles and it wasn't until we opened doors on the outlying settlements that we ran into trouble. The men started stepping into darkness and agents of evil accosted them several times. Violets preparations saved lives this day and all were grateful. The men were learning to be extremely cautious and to return as soon as they realized they were in trouble and I slammed the door shut. We were taking note of all the places the darkness had taken over so we knew where they were and marked it on a map we had laid out on a table. The darkness seemed to be concentrated in the east and fanning out north and south. None of the main Kingdoms were overtaken but outlying areas within those Kingdoms in the east were. It looked as if the Castles were being slowly surrounded, the object being to overtake them. We were going to have to go back and warn them about what was happening in their Kingdoms. They needed what ever chance they could get to survive.

❦

Chapter Fifteen

We were sending the group who went to Castle Lomond in the east who we now knew was being threatened by a high concentration of darkness around it. I opened the door and knew immediately that we were too late. The Dark Man stood in the Great Room of Lomond with the royalty lying in blood all around him with the servants kneeling in that blood. His hat was pulled low and his burning eyes lanced out and through the door toward us. Our three men stumbled back as he lowered his staff and he shot a bolt of fire through the door before I could slam it shut. The fire grazed the arm of one of the men and seared the wall behind him. He fell with a scream clutching his arm and the doctor rushed over to him from where he was attending the injured. He pulled his hand away from the burn to examine it and quickly dropped it when he saw it was bubbling blackly. The burn on the arm and the hand were both bubbling with a black froth that dripped and hardened onto the stone floor. The man continued to scream in agony as we tried to think what to do to stop the burning. The doctor at a loss, called for a pitcher of water which he gently poured over the wound but it continued to bubble. No one moved except a woman who was helping with the wounded dashed out of the room. She then ran back in holding a bowl of flour which she quickly dumped on the bubbling hand and arm. The doctor looked at her in alarm and she shrugged.

"That's how we put out grease fires in the kitchen." She said. "And that looked like a grease fire to me."

The man had stopped screaming and was now moaning in pain. We all looked back at him and realized the fire was indeed out though steam still rose from the wounds. His hand was charred almost to the bone and bone could be seen in his arm. The doctor called for a stretcher and moved him to an isolated area away from other patients while he figured out what to do next.

I looked at the cook and said, "Quick thinking, do you think you could come up with a water proof packet of flour for the men to carry into the field in case someone else gets burned as this man did?"

She blushed and said, "I'm sure the ladies and I could come up with something to be used. We'll get to work on it right away, sir." She hurried away calling to two other women to follow her.

We turned our attention to where the black bubbling stuff had dripped onto the floor. It had stopped burning and hardened on the floor. Dorian suggested a scraper to see if we could scrape it up. A man ran for a metal scraper and being careful not to let the stuff touch our skin we scraped it off the floor and dropped it into a bucket of flour. We sprinkled the floor with flour and placed a chair over it with a sign that said not to move it. Analise had been examining the black mark on the wall and she suggested a paste of flour spread on with a knife. Then later we could figure out if it was dangerous and we could cover it with something more permanent if needed. We spread on a paste made from flour and water and nothing happened though we were careful no one touched it with bare flesh.

The doctor came up to us and said it looked as though the flour had neutralized the fire. He had learned the name of the burned man was Noric. The doctor was going to have to cut away the burned flesh and the remains of the black froth from his hand and arm. Noric was going to be crippled in both left arm and hand if he could save the hand. The other hand he had grabbed the wound with would be saved though it would have limited movement and use. He would know more after the surgery and he healed for a few days.

The five of us met again in the breakfast room with glasses of beer to help calm frayed nerves. It was after midnight and we had to be up early to see the trackers off and be prepared if they needed help.

"At least we know a bit about the Dark Man." I said, and then continued, "We know where he is, Castle Lomond, and that he can shoot some really nasty fire from that staff of his. We know how to stop the burning thanks to our quick thinking cook. The ladies of the castle are making packets of flour for the men to carry in case they or a comrade is burned with that nasty black stuff."

Analise said, "On the down side, he knows where we are. I think if he could open a door himself he would have come after us this night. He must have someone open doors for him and whoever it is is not available. He must have physically taken over Castle Lomond instead of opening a door into the interior. That makes sense since he took over most of the outlying area before taking the castle."

"He killed the royalty and made the servants kneel in the blood," Dorian said, "He is ruthless and knows how to intimidate. I bet he has them all at his beck and call by now if only through fear."

"If they had a chance to stab him in the back they would in a second, if they could get away with it." Violet said.

"They will never get a chance." Georges said.

"Yes, your right they won't," Violet said.

"I have put up a ward so no one can open a door in the castle and all kinds of bells will go off if anyone tries." I said, "We all need to get some sleep and be up at dawn to send off the trackers. We need to be available if they need help."

I rose from my chair and helped Analise from hers. Violet and Georges rose at the same time. Dorian sat for a moment twirling a glass.

"I don't like it. It's to pat, to perfect. I feel like we have been set up. Like we watched a stage set." He said. "He gave us just enough to think we have an advantage, a bit piece of knowledge. I don't like it."

I sighed; I agreed with him I just had not voiced the concern I had. Now it was out in the open and there was not one thing we could do about it. We had to play the game and he had made the first move. At least I had not given him any information on me or us.

"If we play it close to the chest we have the advantage, Dorian." I said, "That is what we must do, close, we give him nothing and when we're ready, we take him down and send him to hell where he belongs. He got very little from us. What he could see was very limited from his side of the door, that's why he hit Noric. The way Noric was dressed he thought he was someone important. He didn't even see the rest of us; we were off to the side. Then I slammed the door shut."

Dorian grunted realizing I had come to the same conclusion he did. He finally got up and we all headed to our rooms and what sleep we could find before daybreak. We needed more information and we hoped the trackers would give us some.

Dawn came quickly and I was already up, dressed and ready to go when Dorian knocked at the door. I opened the door shrugging my arms into my coat. Dorian's eyebrows went up as I pulled the door shut behind me.

"It's important," I said. "Do we have time to grab a coffee and roll?"

"There's a buffet set up in the Great Hall." Dorian answered.

We strode down the halls toward the Great Hall and I asked, "Are the men ready to ride?"

"Their horses are outside the door and the last I saw they were stuffing their faces as if this was their last meal." He said.

We strode into the Hall as the men were finishing up. At least there was coffee and a couple of rolls left that I grabbed off the table as I passed. The men grabbed up their gear and we all went out the Great Doors to where the horses were. The men put on their coats and slung quivers and bows on their backs, swords in scabbards, knives in boots and at belts, throwing stars under belts and packs of flour in pockets easy to reach. They stood by their horses as Dorian and I looked at them. We both wondered if we would see them again.

"Follow the tracks of the beasts to the east and determine where they are or if they went through a door. Take all precautions and don't try to be heroes. This is not hero work." Dorian said.

"Keep your minds open, if you get in trouble I will know and we will be there as fast as we can. I can't read your minds but I can catch what you project, project what you see and we will come prepared. Be wary of the Dark Man go with speed and great care." I said.

We watched them ride off, serious and determined young men bent to their task and fearing they may never return which thankfully would make them cautious. We went back into the castle. I wanted something a little more nourishing to eat and then to sit and concentrate on what the outriders were seeing. I could not help them if I missed what they had to project. Feeling better after some food other then rolls I sat in a chair pulled up to the window and gazed out into the mountains toward where they had ridden.

Chapter Sixteen

My companions sat at a table behind me drinking coffee and talking softly as I concentrated on what was happening out on the trail. I couldn't see only get impressions of what they were seeing. I knew if they got in trouble things would change quickly. They were still tracking when lunchtime came and went. I ate where I sat still listening. I realized something was happening when there was a lot of confusion and conflicting images. They were not sure what they were seeing and I was getting that loud and clear. I was trying to hone in on one vision when all hell broke loose. The trail had stopped then evil erupted out of the ground at their feet.

I stood and said, "We have to go now!"

We were as prepared as we could be. We wore our armor and were armed to the teeth including our bags of flour. Analise ordered the bells to ring as we left the breakfast room. We raced through the Great Hall and out the Great Doors across the courtyard and through the Great Gates of Castle Clarion. The men had heard our call with the ringing of the bells and were ready. A hundred strong and I hoped it was enough as I opened a door into the madness our trackers had stumbled into. Thankful we were prepared and we plunged into the battle and set about stopping the enemy in their tracks. Our outriders were making good work of the beasts and men who seemed to spring from the ground at their feet. The howls and cries of beasts and men were deafening as we sought to destroy and they to overwhelm. Eventually the battle died down and we were able to breath for a bit. Our most important intent was to capture someone we could gain information from. Whoever it was had to be reasonably intelligent and not a beast. We captured several but they were so violent they killed themselves rather then be taken. We finally grabbed two who looked alike and seemed intelligent and at least didn't try to bite our hands off. We chained them together and I asked Georges and Violet to watch over them till we could get back to the castle. Finally the entire enemy was on the ground either dead or dying. We had several who were injured and none who were dead. It was a short battle but we were filthy and weary as we headed back to Castle Clarion. We walked and rode a ways away before I opened a door back to the meadow before the castle. I glanced back to where we had fought and at the men and beasts laying dead their blood soaking into the ground. I wondered what kind of a ruler, if that was what the Dark Man was, could leave his men to be slaughtered and not help them. It was an unthinkable thing to do. I could not leave one man to the fate the Dark Man would give him.

The castle had cells underneath it where we could deposit our prisoners after striping them and dumping buckets of water over them outside the Great Gates. They were filthy and I wanted to be sure they had nothing on them anyone could use to hone in on to make a door inside the castle. I felt the men were random enough they couldn't use them. Once they were relatively clean they looked more alike and I wondered if we had brothers. As I walked around them I saw burn marks on their arms and legs some fresh and stripes where it looked like they had been lashed and lashed hard across their backs. A piece of the left ear was gone on both of them. I walked around them as they squatted and shivered in the snow, I realized they were starving. I could see every rib in their body's and the skulls under their skin. I took a blanket from a man standing by with them and gently wrapped them each in a blanket then ordered them to be taken to their cells and given hot soup with little meat and warm ale.

Dorian, Georges, Violet, Analise and I listen to the report from the head tracker. I realized as we listened to him that we were going to have to start calling them soldiers. We were in a war after all. He told us how the tracks seemed to wander all over like they didn't know where to go. They at least had it together enough to keep a look out on their back trail. They chose a flat open area, dug holes and hid inside waiting for us to catch them up. They sprang out of the earth and snow startling our horses and many of the men and the battle was on.

He said, "My boys did a good job of fending them off and that's when you came in. We are sorely grateful to you for coming to our aid, sir. They are vicious foes and don't seem to care if they get hurt or even killed. They act like they are drugged to take away any feeling they may have no matter how badly they are hurt. They just kept coming at us like they were going to kill us no matter what even if they had to crawl."

"Interesting," I said. "Good observation, Captain." The trackers brows raised in surprise. "Be sure your men are fed and billeted. Are your injured being seen to?" He nodded his head. "Good, when all is in order, choose men and any woman willing to fight to serve under you to the number of thirty-five. Then choose the men or women you believe are best to serve as officers and bring them to me. You are our first troop leader in this war against the Dark Man, choose your people well. You will be our first special attack force as well as our eyes and ears. I want alert people who will survive under undo stress, any questions?"

"No, sir," He said his back straightening where he stood.

"Your name," I asked.

"Jondar, Lee Jondar," He answered.

"You are dismissed, Captain Jondar," I said, as I made a mental note of Captain Jondar's name.

Watching the man walk away Dorian said, "I knew it was coming but it always seemed so far away. Now I know we are at war when our trackers become Captains and our women march to war."

"It is necessary to have a chain of command." I said.

"You are the Commander?" Dorian asked.

I nodded my head, "You and Violet are Generals directly under me. Analise and Georges are Majors under you and Violet." I said, "We will need to set up Lieutenants under the Captains. The Captains will know their men and who best to appoint to positions of responsibility. This war is going to get big enough that if we don't diversify and delegate we will lose because we will muddle around like cattle at the slaughter. I hope the other Kingdoms are coming to the same conclusion. We need to contact the Kingdoms we know are not under the domain of the Dark Man yet and pull them in. If they want to survive they will come."

"Yes, you are right on all counts," Dorian said.

Violet's expression didn't change, she knew what was coming. Analise looked stunned but determined. Georges looked resigned to the fact of actual war and I knew he would come through.

"Analise, would you talk to the Doctor and have him check out our prisoners. I need him to look for a drug that the Dark Man could use to control them and an antidote if there is one. I need to know as soon as possible. Georges, I need you to get a list of all the kingdoms not in the territory of the Dark Man. When Analise gets back we will contact them. Dorian, I need you to sent riders to all the near villages in Clarion and have the people move inside the castle walls, bringing all the food they can carry. Choose a good man to organize housing for them. I'll open a door to those too far away to travel here quickly and pull them through the door." I said and they all rose to go.

I looked at Violet who was still sitting and said, "Violet, I need you to work with Captain Jondar and organize the men and women that are here into groups of thirty-five and assess their fighting skills. Choose the most proficient fighters and set them to training those who are not. We need the best fighters we can get in a short time. Take note of the leaders, we also need scouts who will not get caught. Captain Jondar can help with that since he knows his people."

"Analise if you could find a few servants as you go, and send them in here I'll turn the breakfast room into a War Room." I said. She nodded and turned to leave.

With everyone gone I sat for a few minutes trying not to be overwhelmed. Even with all the training my father had woven into the spell as I slept, at times I still felt like a thirteen year old boy. Violet's voice echoed in my mind, ["You were never a thirteen year old boy, and you are doing what needs to be done for us to survive."] I really need to have a talk with Violet I thought, and got up to convert the breakfast room into a War Room.

CHAPTER SEVENTEEN

Later that night the castle was bursting at the seams with the people from the villages and men training in the fields out side the Postern Gates under new Lieutenants and Captains. We gathered in the War Room, having been the Breakfast Room it was easy to have food brought in. We talked as we ate. The Doctor had discovered the men we had captured had been ingesting a drug in what food they were given. They were starving and in poor shape, proving the Dark Man believed his men disposable or he just didn't care. The Doctor had given them each an antidote he hoped would work in the food they were eating here. They were eating plenty of a meaty broth and fresh water as starving men will. They were passing a black sludge with a foul smell that required constant removal and burying. He thought we would be able to question them in the morning when they would be free of the Dark Man's influence.

The other Kingdoms had seen the wisdom in bringing their people inside their castle walls and to start training for war. They had all agreed to my command. We had accomplished what we needed to do this day and our next decision waited on what we would learn from our prisoners in the morning. We needed to get good nights sleep. Dorian had set sentries and I had put up wards to warn us if anything came near the castle during the night. They all rose to go to their rooms except Violet. It was time we had our talk it had been put off long enough.

I poured us each a fresh cup of coffee and then I asked, "Violet what do you know?"

She sighed, and then said, ["Dad knew you and I were alike. The youngest and the oldest of his children, we compliment each other. We can work with and through each other, helping and enhancing our abilities to accomplish our goals. We have the same goals simply because we are the same, we have no choice. Dad sent you to the Island of Dreams and me to the Place of Assassins. We have both been saturated in diplomacy and fighting skills. We were meant to lead and we were meant to save the World of Light as we know it, though not necessarily this planet. Our natural enemy is the Dark Man and you and I together have the skills to defeat him."]

["How can I hear you in my head?"] I asked.

["It is a gift few have. Father knew we had the gift, as you and Analise can talk to each other, you and I can we just need to remember to use our doors for privacy. There will probably be others we can also talk to."] She said, ["Actually you have not realized it but this entire conversation has been done in our heads. You asked the first question out loud and I answered telepathically and that's how we continued."]

I thought about that and realized she was right; we were so in tune I did not even notice? What else could we do? Could we open other doors in our heads?

["Yes we can,"] Violet said, ["You forgot to shut your door so I heard everything, where do you want to open doors and why?"]

["The Kings of the other Kingdoms should be in on the interview with our prisoners. They need to know what the black man is doing to the people of our lands."] I said.

["Good idea, I can open doors and you can talk to them then conduct the interview with them watching through me."] She said. ["We should contact them tonight to warn them about the interview in the morning so we don't waste a lot of time explaining then."]

That's what we did for several hours that night and got to bed late. We had everything set up for the morning. The only change was I needed to open doors also, so many were interested in what the prisoners had to say. All we needed to do was explain it all to the rest of the command team. Before we went to our rooms Violet said, "Your door is the red front door to our home in the mountains with the brass knocker."

I said, "Yes." She turned and walked away.

The night had been quiet, and we were eating breakfast when the Doctor came in to advise us on our prisoners.

"They had a rough night," He said, "It seems the drug they were ingesting was very painful as it has been flushed from their system. I have started them on soft food, porridge and soft biscuits with honey along with the meat broth. The drug affected their minds because they recall things now they have done they would not normally have done. They are not only weak physically but emotionally devastated by what they have remembered."

"Can we question them?" I asked.

"Yes you can but you should know that my observation shows the only reason they were serving the black man is the drugs. They are just poor farm folks who don't even know how to fight, forced to serve a man they hate." He said. "They are bathed, have clean clothes and are under guard in the questioning room on the cell level."

"Is there a table in the questioning room?" I asked.

"Yes and four chairs, two occupied by the prisoners." He said.

"Please bring in three more chairs and put them along the wall behind the two men." I said.

Violet and I had explained to everyone what we had accomplished last night and how the interview was to be set up. With them sitting behind the prisoners the Kings could see them from our doors and know we were who we said we were. A good precaution, we had also searched their Kingdoms telepathically to be sure they had not been compromised. Georges and Dorian had a hard time understanding doors in our minds that the Kings would observe through but finally took our word for it. Analise understood perfectly.

We all filed into the room, Violet and I sitting in front of the prisoners the rest sitting behind with Analise in the middle. I insisted on this precaution in case things got out of control Analise could be protected easier. I looked at these men for the first time since they were put in the cells. I would not have believed they were the same men. One was openly crying with his face on the table. The other one sat and stared straight ahead as if we were not there. As I sat there I wondered how we were going to question these men. Violet answered, ["carefully"]. I glanced at her, I could see the doors open in her eyes and opened the doors in mine looking again at the prisoners.

"Can you hear us?" I asked. And got no response, I leaned forward and rapped on the table. The man who was crying jerked up and warily eyed us with tears still streaming down his face, still no response from the other.

"What is your name?" I asked.

"Jims Donegal," He said.

"Where are you from?" I asked.

"Lenville outside Castle Lomond, it's just a little place with orchards." Jims said.

"Is that where you joined the Dark Man?" I asked.

"The Dark Man, is that what he is? I didn't join, he just takes. Whatever he wants, he takes." Jims said.

"How does he take, Jims?" I asked.

"I don't know, some men come into town and they buys drinks all around and it did taste funny. I told some of the guys it tastes funny. They said you complaining about free beer? And you know, you can't complain about free beer. Can you? Next thing you know he takes what ever he wants and we don't complain cause you know, its free beer."

"What does he take Jims?" I ask.

"Women, he takes women for his men and you know we don't complain. Sisters and daughters and wives, he took my Sally and I didn't complain. He made me kill my kids, lil' Jenny and Leo named for Sally's dad. I slit their throats as Sally screamed at me and still I did it, he told me to so I did. It was better I slit their throats then have happen what I saw happen to other kids. Just little kids with their bums ripped out and the big men laughing. Their da's and Gr'da's doin that and killin em, stringing them up from trees and watchin them danglin and choking. The women screamin, cryin and fightin, their ma's fighten and if they fought hard enough they'd get sent with their kids. They hauled all the women away even some of the older ones to cook for them. Most of the older ones they just killed smashed their heads in to save their swords. Took all our food too from the villages, left anyone still there to starve. Wasn't many left. He took the men to fight though we don't know how to fight never fought just farmed, he wanted us to kill and we did, climbed over each other to kill and do his bidin. He took everything. Set what was left to fire. All gone all gone all gone.

"Do you know this man next to you?" I asked.

"Nah, don't know nobody. We just got grouped together and sent out don't even know where. Where are we anyways?" Jims asked.

"Do you know why you are fighting," I asked Jims.

"To kill, kill, kill the whole world to burn and maim but mostly to kill." Jims answered.

I knocked on the table in front of the man who just stared and said, "Sir, can you hear me? Who are you? Where did you come from?" I asked.

Violet said, ["Don't touch him."]

I reached out my hand toward him and he growled at me deep in his throat.

"Touch me and die," He said. He never stopped staring straight ahead.

Violet said, ["I told you not to touch him."]

["I didn't."] I said.

["Close enough."] She responded.

We both looked at the silent man and saw his eyes turn red, a red that burned the flesh around his eyes. It started to burn turning the skin black making his eyes look like holes. A voice pushed its way out of this mans throat ripping and tearing its way out. A voice that was not his spoke, though his mouth did not move.

"So you are the one who seeks to stop me. A blue eyes I see. What can a little upstart like you do against me who already owns half of the world and will own the rest very soon?" The voice said.

"Dark Man, what do you want with our world? We are a peaceful world." I asked.

"Not anymore its not. The true nature of your people is coming out. They want to rip, roar and burn the whole world. Kill, kill, kill that's what they want and I do try to keep them happy. And they will be so happy when you die. You can not hide from me. I will personally rip your tongue out and listen to your blood gurgle as you try to scream. And that woman beside you she will die and I will make it long and painful." The Dark Man hissed leaning forward in his chair. "You will watch, you will try to scream and won't be able to. I will put your eyes out before she dies so you never know what happens to her and it can haunt you the rest of the short life I will let you live before I kill you."

Jims started to scream a high pitched strangled scream. He lunged for the silent man the Dark Man was speaking through and grabbing his hair banged his head on the table over and over. Analise stood up, Georges and Dorian stood up and in front of her. They tried to help the soldiers as they tried to pull Jims off and could not. Jims jerked the man's head back hard enough that we heard a crack then he jammed his first two fingers into the red eyes as far as they would go. He threw his own head back howling and dropped over the silent man he had just killed in a dead faint and slid to the floor. Both Violet and I were standing looking down; it's amazing how quickly it all happened. Analise looked up and straight into our eyes.

Chapter Eighteen

"Do you see what we all have to deal with? Did you hear what this poor man lived? Did you hear how whole towns and Kingdoms have died? Do you want this for your mothers, daughters, children and babes? Do you want your men to be turned into such animals that they want to kill? Will kill to kill, with drugs. Where is your water supply? Do Not Dither, come to arms and help us defeat the Dark Man!" She said. I could feel the chaos behind the doors as the kings reacted to what happened. I realized she was talking to the Kings looking out of my and Violets eyes and I knew they would all join in the fight against the Dark Man.

"I wanted to know, I needed to know what we faced. What the evil was that is invading the world. How we were going to combat this evil," I said, as we sat in the War Room just after noon. "This evil I have seen, I wish I didn't know or didn't have to deal with it. Better yet that it just didn't exist, and all the children had to worry about was being stung by a bee when they picked a flower. My god, the evil of that man is horrendous. We must find a way to stop him before the whole world is devastated"

My four companions and I sat and contemplated what we had heard that morning. None of us could eat lunch so we sat and drank coffee. We even looked at that speculatively after what Analise said about water source and drugs. The man Jims was back in his cell completely unresponsive and according to the doctor he may never wake up. After his diatribe it may be better if he doesn't. I would not want to live with his memories or a future with the Dark Man.

"Our water source is inside the castle walls." Analise said, "Even though we live with ice and snow in the spring thaws it melts and fills huge natural aquifers deep under the ground and then it comes up in artesian wells we have capped. Turn a valve and we have all the water pressure we need and it cannot be compromised outside the castle walls. The wells are the reason Castle Clarion was built on this site."

"How many wells are there? Who knows about them?" I asked.

"Three, placed at intervals in the castle. Anyone could know where they are they have never been kept secret." She answered.

I stood and said, "Guards, they need to be guarded now. Six to a well and change the guard every six hours. The guards need to know why they guard the water supply and that all our lives depend on their diligence."

Dorian was at the door and calling to a Lieutenant in the great room. When he arrived we explained what we needed, guards for the water supply and why, he moved quickly to see it done.

Dorian then said, "There are shut offs at each well head, we need to limit water flowing through pipes. Water can be stored in barrels and tested before use but we need to shut off the water during low use times such as at night when the majority are sleeping. It will be inconvenient but safe."

"Yes," I said, "Sunrise to sunset the water will be on but we need to vary by as much as a half hour when they are shut off or turned on. Precise times can be compromised."

"Two men, John and Owen accompanied by four soldiers will get the job done. I will personally go and talk to them; they can be counted on to keep the water safe." Dorian said.

We had all our people from the furthest villages inside the walls and everyone seemed to be in good spirits and confident we would prevail. Wards were set to go off incase someone tried to breach our walls. The army was being trained by our best fighters. The water supply was being protected in case we had infiltrators. We have warned the other Kingdoms and they were preparing to back us up when we called. They were terrified by what they saw and heard through Jims Donegal what the Dark Man could do and were determined to fight. We had done what we could to prepare our defenses and the other Kingdoms were working on there's. Now we needed a plan to attack to defeat the Dark Man.

Four of us sat in the breakfast room turned War Room talking about what we knew and how we need to go about crushing the Dark Man. At this time we had ten Captains with fifty men and women under them being trained and training others to fight the Dark Man. We knew as more were trained we would need more captains but we decided to pull the established Captains into the War Room and do some brainstorming.

Dorian returned bringing John and Owen with him. "I have talked with John and Owen; they understand the importance of keeping the water supply safe and are honored to take responsibility for it."

I rose and regarded both men who stood stiffly at attention. "Water Wardens are who you are. No one has authority over you except us five in this room and two of us must be present to make changes in the water rules we will set up. You are honor bound to protect the water at all cost. You will have sixty-eight men and women under you command, six people on eight hour shifts at each well and four will be with you when the well is either turned on or off. We have temporary guards at the wells now, choose your people well, the safety of the water means we live or we die." The Black Sword started to hum at my side. I pulled it from its scabbard and knew instantly what it wanted. I raised the sword and touched each man on their right shoulder. As the sword touched each man three descending bright blue drops of water appeared under their right eye. I sheathed the sword.

"No one will refute the authority of the water given by the Black Sword." I said. To their credit neither one flinched when I pulled and touched them so close to the neck with the sword, I knew we had chosen the right men, the sword approved.

John and Owen left to set up their command over the water and we went back to discussing how to defeat the Dark Man.

"Now that we have the water shielded," The Black Sword started to hum and I paused. Everyone looked at me expectantly so I pulled the sword from its scabbard and held it up. Immediately we were surrounded by a shimmering blue bubble. We looked at each other then Violet picked up a roll and threw it at the bubble. The roll went through and landed on the floor.

"OK and this helps how?" Dorian asked.

Violet stood there perplexed then said, "Wait." She dashed to the shield slowing down as she slid through it. She picked up the roll turned threw it at us and it bounced off the shield.

"A shield," I said, "I wonder how much we can cover with it."

Dorian stood and said excitedly, "Let's go outside and find out!"

"Violet," I asked, "Can you come back through?"

Violet walked up to the shield and with no fear laid her hand upon it and was immediately thrown up and back to land on her back on the floor.

She slowly rose up on one elbow and said, "I don't recommend trying to go through the shield it packs a hell of a punch." She then lay back down. Georges was through the shield before I could bring it down and was kneeling next to Violet rubbing her hand when the rest of us stood over her to be sure she was OK. I called for the doctor who arrived quickly and examined Violet.

"We all have an electrical currant that keeps our systems running in time and it seems that Violets has been interrupted. However briefly this current is interrupted it takes a short time for it to reset. She should be fine in a short while." The doctor said, "Though if she had a heart problem she would be dead by now."

We all looked at each other realizing what this could mean for us. Knocking the enemy down and killing them when they could not touch us. Everyone would have to stay inside the shield and Dorian was right we needed to see how much it would cover. We also needed to know if we could lean out of the shield and come back in if we don't completely go out as Violet had.

"OK, time to experiment. Violet do you think you can walk outside or would you like Georges to carry you?" I asked innocently.

Violet scowled at me and said, "I damn well can get there on my own power!" she said struggling to get up. When she got to her feet Georges smiled and gallantly offered her his arm. How could she refuse, she even leaned on him a bit which we all ignored.

We went out the Postern Gate where the men and women were in training. We gathered Captains together who had troops practicing on the field and explained what we wanted to do. They looked at us disbelieving until I unsheathed the Black Sword and put a shield around our small gathering. These tough men were fascinated by what they saw and wanted to reach out and touch it. We explained what happened to Violet, how she was able to go through the shield but could not come back in and we wanted to know if someone could go half way out and back in.

Captain Jondar said, "Well let's see if we can." He walked up to the shield put his hand out through the shield then drew it back in. He then put his arm through and drew it back in. He continued with his head, which was scary, his entire upper body, his upper body and one leg and finally all but one foot went through and he was able to come back in. He chose not to try to come back in when he was completely outside the shield after hearing what happened to Violet. Violet had a tough reputation among the soldiers and he didn't want to get knocked on his butt if that's what happened to her. We all stood fascinated by his antics and we now knew a lot more about the shield. The rest of the soldiers had stopped to watch us so we explained to them about the shield and that we wanted to see how many people it could protect. The Black Sword must have understood because we were all suddenly standing under a dome of blue.

"OK then it seems to cover whatever we need it to cover." I said. "Let's split into two groups and have one group attack the shield."

The soldiers moved apart and the shield adjusted itself to cover half of the soldiers. The other half shot arrows, slings, and spears and hit the shield with swords. All were ineffective except those who hit it with swords were thrown onto their backs and lay twitching on the ground. That stopped the sword fighters. Everyone was amazed. We then had the soldiers in the shield shoot arrows, throw slings and spears through the shield and they went right through landing on the ground outside. Those with swords could lean out hack at the enemy and come back in and be protected as long as they did not step out completely. The few who did step out and tried to come back in were thrown on their backs and lay twitching on the ground. Everyone was learning. We switched sides and practiced with both halves inside and outside the shield. We realized we were going to have to do this with the entire army and quickly. The Dark Man was waiting for no one and the longer we waited before attacking the more people would be lost to him.

Chapter Nineteen

In our excitement over the shield we had missed the noon meal so we gathered in the War Room and ordered food to be brought. We were planning on working with the troops through the evening and much of the night. Waiting for our food we quickly opened doors into the other Kingdoms to get updates. The most eastern Kingdoms furthest outlying villages were being swallowed by the Dark Man. Some of the castles were almost surrounded by him and most of their people were inside the Castle walls and the walls had not been breached. It would be a massacre if the Dark Man and his monsters got in. We needed to move and move quickly.

We called all the troops onto the field as soon as everyone had eaten. The word had spread about the shield so everyone was expecting something to happen. All the troops were told to march as I drew the Black Sword marching in the middle of them all. I could see men all around me looking up and around at the blue surrounding them with mouths hanging open but still marching. The shield moved with us so now we knew we could cover ground and stay protected. The only thing we did not know was if it would repel the black stuff the Dark Man could throw that stuck and burned. As I said that the Swords hum intensified and I had a feeling it would repel anything it needed to repel, and my confidence soared. We broke up early, ate and went to bed. We had decided I would open a door at 4 am, which meant we had to be up and ready to go by 3:30 and I needed to sleep. We were going to hit the most overrun areas and I hoped we would find the Dark Man so we could end this. After eating all I could hold I headed to bed falling face first into its comfy softness fully clothed, after all I had to be up in just a few hours. There was a banging on my door, Dorian.

I felt like it had only been a few minutes but I got up and stumbled to the door and opened it. It had been only a few minutes and there stood Analise fully dressed in her battle clothes.

"It's 3:00 already?" I asked.

"No, but I couldn't sleep, I well, I, couldn't sleep alone. I'm scared, I think." She replied confused. She looked like she couldn't believe she was here at my door. I pulled her into my arms her head on my shoulder and rested my head on her soft red hair.

"Come on Ana," I said unconsciously shortening her name. "No one should be alone on the eve of battle." I led her to my bed and we both climbed on top fully clothed, I wrapped her in my arms breathing in the wonder of her with my face buried in her hair and we fell deeply asleep until the banging on my door at 3:00.

For some reason I woke to the banging wondering what green eyes flecked with gold meant because I had not seen any others then those belonging to the girl I held in my arms. Wait, girl I held in my arms, Dorian, shit. Well into the fire, and I rolled out of bed after disentangling my self from the princess. She sat up groggily while I answered the door, it was Dorian.

"It is time for you and the princess to rise; we must eat before we travel." He said after eyeing my fully dressed state with approval. He nodded to Analise as she stumbled to the bathroom obviously fully dressed and strode down the hall as I stood looking after him.

As we were walking to the Great Hall I casually said, "Dorian didn't seem too upset or surprised you were in my room with me."

After glancing at me curiously she said, "Do you think I would go anywhere with out telling Dorian, he would skin me alive if he didn't know where I was. He likes you and he knows you are a gentleman to the core. He knew I needed to be near you and what I need is very important to Dorian."

"Hmmm, nice. So that's why he didn't kill me." I said and I meant it, it was nice, she just laughed. "What do green eyes flecked with gold mean? I have seen no others then yours, only varying shades of brown."

"You truly do not know?" She asked, "Only Royalty have green eyes flecked with gold, it means we were born to lead. We have the innate ability to make choices for great numbers of people and lead them on paths for the benefit of all involved, our Kingdom."

"Does that mean all the Royalty in all the kingdoms have green eyes?" I asked.

"Unfortunately no, true Royalty has slowly died out or been killed over the decades and are as rare as your blue eyes. Many of the Kingdoms are governed by a plain green or even muddy green eyes and sometimes brown who are not truly meant to govern a Kingdom. They don't have the innate ability to lead, choose good advisors or champions for their cause. That is why so many have dithered in the face of the Dark Man and others have been completely overrun, they are not true leaders." Analise said,

"I believe it may be time for a change." I said.

Analise looked at me questioningly as we rounded the corner into the entrance to the Great Hall just as Violet and Georges came from the other direction. I briefly wondered where they had spent the night and if they had spent the night in each others arms should I have brotherly concern? A laser beam of thought bore into my head, ["Don't even think about it, brother."] OK, that took care of that.

We all nodded to each other and entered the Great hall. Everyone who could cram themselves into it was there and the Great Doors were thrown open where more soldiers were crowded on the steps and courtyard below. Everyone was cramming food into their mouths; when you march into a war you never know when you'll get your next meal. Even though every soldier is provided with a pack with food it is hard tack and it could always be lost in battle. It is important to eat as much as possible to sustain you as long as possible. Wars have been lost by the lack of food. There was a great air of expectancy as every one of the men stopped and looked up as we entered the room. Dorian was to our right inside the doors; he looked at me with raised eyebrow. Violet and Georges were to my left as I bowed to Analise.

"My Princess," I said, "You are up." I took her hand and guided her up onto a chair and then onto the top of the nearest table, the four of us taking our places standing on the floor behind her. She stood there tall and regal in her battle dress, sword swinging at her side, red hair cascading down her back. Her green eyes glinting with gold flashing as she surveyed the soldiers.

"This day," she began, "We march on the Dark Man. We as one body, one mind, one soul will prevail. We march for our right to live, we march for the light. The Dark Man will fall under our swords and burn in fire as we set our people free." She raised her fist, "We will live free in the light, it is our destiny, fight for the light, live in the light. Fight for the light, live in the light." The throng of soldiers took up the chant and it spread out the doors into the crowd and up into the early morning sky. I pulled the Black Sword that was humming and raised it behind the Princess and she was infolded in a blue sparkling light that surged and crackled as the chant rose in fervor.

"Fight for the light, live in the light." The chant for our lives rang out across the land and was heard in the furthest reaches of the kingdoms. Many across the land stopped to listen and took up the chant, we were ready to fight and we had put the Dark Man on notice.

As Analise jumped off the table I realized we could use individual shields and started to consider; how could we use them. How many could we, the Black Sword and I make and sustain. Its power seemed to be endless and I was anxious to find out just what we could do. We contacted the other Kingdoms who were ready as they could be in such a short time to lend a hand to the battle. We briefed them as well as possible on the shield and told them to spread the word among their troops so there would be as few surprises as possible. Even an idea of what they would encounter would be better then no warning at all.

We gathered in the big meadow below the castle. I was going to open a gate a few miles from the village where there was a large concentration of the Dark Mans monsters. We were hoping to find the Dark Man himself but I had my doubts. If he had someone opening doors for him he could be anywhere and not show himself until we were weary from battle. We needed a strategy to find him quickly before that happened. The stars shone in the morning sky like diamonds as I opened a long door high enough for the horses to go through. We stood looking into a large meadow where the morning sun was slowly burning off the frost. It looked so peaceful until we saw the columns of black oily smoke rising into the sky beyond a copse of trees. Quiet and the element of surprise were of the utmost importance if we were to make the greatest impact. The shield wasn't going to work going through the trees so we slowly advanced through the door and wove through the trees. The acrid smoke got stronger the closer we got to it and whatever was burning. I got the strongest feeling we were too late. Violet said, ["We are too late."]

CHAPTER TWENTY

We came out of the trees and into the village with other soldiers joining us from other doors. All we found was devastation. It was just as Jims Donegal said in the prison below the castle, everyone left was dead and they didn't die easily. There were mostly old men, women, small children and babies. They were hanging in trees and thrown in huge piles. I could hear men retching behind me and I had to swallow hard a few times. Those next to me were doing the same thing I was and they looked green, it was probably a reflection of my own face. Analise and Violet stood still as statues, shocked with tears streamed down their faces. I could hear soldiers crying openly and asking why. Why indeed, it had been left to have the fullest possible affect on us, to dishearten us so we would turn around and give up. It had the opposite effect on me; I thought, NO NEVER AGAIN, this can never happen again. The Dark Man has to be stopped now.

I turned to my left and said, "Dorian set Details to digging mass graves in the meadow. Details to look in the building left standing for shrouds. I need a Detail with me to cut these poor souls down; we will not leave them like this for the birds to peck. Lets suck it up and get it done quickly we need to find the bastard who did this to these people."

Dorian looked relieved to turn away from the sight before us, turning Analise and Violet with him so they had a chance to re-coup. He started calling out and soldiers stepped up to volunteer. I quickly had fifteen men at my side holding knives. Dorian had set up guards and look outs so we could not be taken by surprise and we set to work. The shroud Detail was bringing sheets and blankets, bags and pillow cases, curtains from windows anything we could use to wrap the dead in. We cut down a body and they gently wrapped them up and set them aside to be transported to the meadow for burial. Soldiers were gently lifting bodies off the piles sorting them out with the same care they would give their mothers, fathers or babes. Many had tears streaming down their faces they didn't bother to wipe off as they silently worked wrapping each one with tenderness. Analise and Violet were helping wrap the babes and crying openly with each child they enfolded. The Dark Man had not treated them tenderly but by god we would.

Suddenly a soldier cried out and I turned expecting to see that he had found someone he knew. He stood holding a small child from one of the piles of dead in his arms with a look of total astonishment on his face and I could see the child was moving, not moving much but moving.

"Analise," I cried as I moved toward the soldier. "Analise we need you now, here, we need you now!" She looked up and started to run toward us.

"Oh my god, oh my god," she cried grabbing my shoulder, "Trevor we have to get this child back to the castle right now. The doctor can save her, I know he can." I opened a door right there into the Great Room of Castle Clarion where people turned in surprise to see a door appear and what they could see through that door. We could hear gasps and cries of dismay and horror as the people in the castle looked through toward us. The soldier who found the child refused to let it go so he went with Analise and they stepped through the door and into the waiting arms of the doctor. I closed the door and turned back to the task at hand, those on the other side would have to live with what they saw as we would. Everyone was galvanized, they had found a survivor and it was as if everyone had found the child. Great caution was used from now on incase there was another alive somewhere in all the death.

It went quicker then I thought when I first saw what was before us. In a short time all the dead were accounted for in the village. It had been scoured in hopes of another survivor but the Dark Man had been thorough and no one else was found alive. We stood looking at all the shroud wrapped bodies and the daunting job of transporting them to their graves. The Black Sword started to hum so I pulled it from its scabbard at my side. It started to hum louder as we stood and wondered what the sword could or would do. The blue energy that comprised its shield shot from it and enfolded the first body in the long line of bodies we had laid out. The body rose from the ground as the energy moved on enveloping each body in turn. A slow procession of dead transported by the Black Sword passed us by on the way to their graves. We all stood wide eyed as the bodies floated by us and we could hear startled exclamations from the look outs in the woods and the men in the meadow where the graves were being dug. The Black Sword was doing its part by showing respect to the dead and transporting them in honor.

We followed the last body as it was lifted from the ground. We arrived at the burial site as the last body was being lay to rest with its companions in neat rows in the graves. Every shovel available had a willing hand to cover them in their last resting place. Every shovel was passed hand to hand since everyone wanted to be a part of covering these poor souls in their eternal beds. At last it was done but the Black Sword was not done. I had held it at my side as the burying was done, to sheath it seemed disrespectful it deserved to see it well done. The sword started to sing as I held it aloft and everyone stood staring at the huge grave before us. Our tears had dried and we stood as if stunned by the gravity of what lay before us. The Black Sword sang and the ground trembled as a huge rock rose from the depths of the earth at the midpoint of the mass grave. Writing began to appear on the rock grooved deep to last an eternity. The Sword sang on and on coming to a last sweet note as if singing a lullaby to a dear child and falling silent. I circled the grave coming to a stop before the rock and I read out loud;

These sweet souls
Taken from us so soon
In terror and in tears
We consign with love
To the meadow so sweet
To flowers and bees
Gentle summer rains
Soft winter snows
Never to be forgotten
Remembered always
Sleep and rest
We are here

As I read the last line the Black Sword sang one last time in the meadow. The grave trembled slightly as grass began to grow lush and green, it was filled with every kind wildflower and the smell was as sweet as the first rain. All of our hearts were warmed as we started back to our respective castles. The grave appeared to be covered with a beautiful quilt made by someone who dearly loved those snuggled under it. From that time onward it always looked beautiful no matter the season.

We filed back through our doors to ready ourselves for the battle we were all ready to fight. The Dark Man had inspired us, we all wanted him dead.

⸻ ❧ ⸻

CHAPTER TWENTY-ONE

The first thing I did as well as Dorian, Violet and Georges was look for Analise and the child who survived. We were told by the first person who saw us that they were in the first small bedroom off the right hall from the Great Room. We all headed in that direction and found the Doctor, Analise and the soldier with the child in the room. Analise looked happy, the soldier relieved and the doctor satisfied.

"What's happening?" I asked with everyone crowding at my back.

The Doctor turned and said, "It seems someone drugged our young lady here," he smoothed back her hair, "so she would appear dead and not be killed. You would have to check closely to know she still lived, so was passed by. She should be fine once the drug works out of her system otherwise there is nothing wrong with her. I believe she was drugged before serious fighting and killing broke out in the village so she probably won't even have any memory of what befell those poor people. Someone loved this little tyke enough to take a chance at drugging her, but the alternative was certainly worse."

We all stood stunned, she was fine and hopefully did not even have any bad memories. All those dead and this one little girl of all her people lived. What a legacy she had. We heard a soft mewing sound and we all looked at the bed the child lay in. She was so small she couldn't be more then eighteen months old and so sweet with golden blond curls that lay plastered to her small head as it turned back and forth as she tried to wake up. She gave a small cry as she opened her eyes so big and a startling blue it took all our breaths away. Blue eyes, she had blue eyes that gazed steadily into my own as she raised her chubby little arms to me to be picked up. I looked at the doctor and he nodded his head. I bent down picked her up and she snuggled into my arms. Violet was openly crying, and Violet does not cry. Everyone else was immobile with surprise except the doctor.

"It looks like my work here is done," he said, "Be sure she is fed, milk and a meat broth to start to flush the residual drug from her system. I'm sure you all know how to take care of a baby. If she has any problems call me immediately, it's not every day I get to see a miracle."

As the doctor left everyone sprang into action. Violet had stopped crying and coaxed the baby from me which wasn't hard with her blue eyes. Dorian stepped out and called for milk and broth in bottles for the baby. The soldier asked to be excused to go back to his unit with the request to see the baby again, his name Brian Hopewell. We sent him off with an affirmative yes.

As he was leaving Analise said, "Hope," he paused with a question in his eyes.

"Her name is Hope," He left with a big smile on his face. We learned at a later time that is what everyone called him, Hope.

Hope laughed, Violet laughed the first spontaneous happy sound I had heard from her in twelve years. Analise laughed and then we were all laughing as the milk and broth arrived. Dorian and Georges excused themselves to see the troops. I knew we had to check in with the other Kingdoms and find the Dark Man but I was loath to leave this bit of happiness amid so much sadness. I watched as Violet and Analise took turns holding and feeding the baby, they snuggled and giggled as only women can do. I contemplated Violets outburst of tears realizing how much she and

Hope had in common both losing their parents to violence at a very young age. What was the fate of Hopes parents? Surely they or at least one of them had blue eyes, I hoped for their sake the Dark Man did not know about them and they were mercifully dead.

"Hope Violet Analise Dawson," I proclaimed and they both looked at me questioning. "Hope because that is what she is. Violet and Analise because that is who you are and she will grow to love and be like both of you, Dawson because she has blue eyes as only the truth can."

They both nodded and I excused myself. I had someone to find and to kill.

I found Dorian and Georges in the War Room. Since Dorian knew the castle and the people in it I asked him if he would find a nursemaid for Hope. Someone loving who could also teach and protect her, he thought a minute and said he knew just the person. He left and after a few minutes came back with a slim young woman with dark eyes and a long dark braid down her back who he introduced as Jasmine. She is the cook's daughter, oldest of five and a widow. She was trained as a soldier but chose to stay by her aging mother side. When I asked her if she would be willing to look after Hope she beamed with anticipation.

Her greatest sorrow was never having a child with her husband before he died and would love to be Hopes nursemaid. Though she wanted to be near her mother she certainly was not old enough to need Jasmines constant care. I agreed, I had met the head cook and she was anything but helpless. This way she could be in the castle near her mother but out of her hair as her mother put it, and she loved children. I liked and approved of her so I told her where to find Hope with Violet and Analise. This was a kind of test, if she could ingratiate herself with Violet and Analise she was the woman we needed for Hope.

I turned my attention back to finding the Dark Man. I opened doors and Dorian and Georges talked to the neighboring Kingdoms searching for clues as to where he was. There were rumors but we needed hard facts. I wanted him found and dead. He seemed to have a talent with smoke and mirrors, leading people to believe one thing when another was true. We narrowed it down to Castle Laird. The village he decimated earlier this day was one of its outlaying villages. The villagers thought they were far enough away from the castle to escape notice and had not gone to the protection of its walls. They had paid a heavy price. The Dark Man had continued on toward Castle Laird and was preparing to attack the castle.

Everyone was shifting into high gear as Violet and Analise walked into the room. It seems Jasmine made an impression, she was someone Analise knew from childhood and she herself could not have picked a better woman to take care of Hope. We had our team back and we set to work. It had been a long day and even though we knew the attack on Castle Laird could start at any moment we needed to eat and rest a few hours. We would be no help if we were falling down with exhaustion. We ordered everyone to eat to their fill and sleep; we would march in four hours, again with the stars that looked like diamonds in the black sky.

CHAPTER TWENTY-TWO

I crammed food and fell into bed this time alone, only to get up and cram more food. The short sleep did wonders for all of us. I opened a small window into the area around Castle Laird and saw the entire castle surrounded by a screaming hoard of mad men and monsters. There were huge fires burning on the ramparts of the castle in large pits. Big cauldrons of what looked like oil was being heated and dumped onto the enemy below. Then archers with burning arrows were shooting into it and setting it on fire. We saw the monsters we had seen before burst into flames and burn with an oily smoke. The fires were also letting the men defending the castle to see their attacker where there were no pillars of smoke. But it also made them visible. Over all there was lightening in the sky as the Dark Man threw his bolts of black sludge that stuck and burned. The Dark Man was here.

We quickly contacted the other Kingdoms and set a plan in action. We would all come through doors behind the enemy surrounding them and pressing them between us and the castle walls. We would move forward slaughtering the enemy in search of the Dark Man. Whoever found him would shoot arrows dipped in a chemical that burned green into the air. Then select groups would converge on that area as the rest continued fighting. The

Dark Man must die and the quicker he did the more we could save. The savage men could be detoxified of the drug that controlled them though many of them would choose to die instead of living with what they had done when they remembered. They still deserved a chance.

Dressed in our armor I opened a door and we swept into the field behind the enemy as the other Kingdoms did the same. Suddenly there was a great army behind and completely surrounding the enemy. Unless the Dark Man could fly, we had him trapped. We started to advance and the Black Sword began to hum and I drew it from its scabbard. The hoard in front of us was noticing us and turning to fight. The shield lifted from the Black Sword and swept around the entire circle. I saw some surprised looks on soldiers who had not experienced the shield but they held their place and continued to march forward. Spears and arrows bounced off the shield and we could hear cheers come up from the men behind the shield. The enemy tried attacking the shield itself only to be thrown back twitching on the ground to be easily dispatched by someone leaning through the shield to slice with sword or ax. We lost a few men who stepped through too far and not being able to return were left exposed and quickly hacked to pieces. The soldiers learned real fast to watch where and how far they were stepping. Our archers behind the shields were having a tremendous affect on the enemy as they shot their arrows and their targets fell to the ground to be trampled under foot. We were slaughtering them with little danger to ourselves. Our flaming arrows were finding the monsters and they were bursting into oily flames making an eerie light. I knew the Dark Man would not let this continue; he had to have something up his sleeve.

I heard shouting behind us and turned to see another faction of the enemy coming onto our flank. How big was the Dark Mans army I thought as we were attacked from behind by savage men screaming and monsters howling. Part of the army turned to counter this new threat and attacked in return. We were now sandwiched between the Dark Mans army and it became imperative we find him and quickly. The Black Swords shield held to the front but we were exposed to the back. We would have to defend ourselves and repel the attack from behind without a shield, continue forward and search for the Dark Man.

I suddenly saw green arrows fly high into the air in the midst of the heaviest lightning concentration. I made a choice and dropped the shield choosing to shield the groups designated to find and kill the Dark Man. Evidence of small shields converging on the area the green arrows were shot from could be seen through out our army. A shielded group from every Kingdom was heading as straight as possible for the Dark Man. The army instead of discouraged by this turn of event took courage and surged with renewed vigor into the enemy hacking and killing with renewed vigor.

Our group consisting fifty of our best fighting men including me, Dorian, Georges, Violet and Analise were sloughing through pools of blood and body parts. Using our shield to propel our way through the enemy throwing them up and out of the way to twitch on the ground, we did not pause to kill them. Our aim was the Dark Man and I knew he wanted me as dead as much as I wanted him dead. I knew this would come down to us two and I was ready to step up and put him down. Violet spoke, ["Do not be over confident brother that could be your downfall."] Abashed I knew she was right, he was not going to stand there and let me kill him. His followers would also be willing to slit my throat or stab me in the back. I answered, ["When it comes down to the two of us as you know it must, you need to keep my back and I will promise not be overconfident. He is a tricky one I know."] ["I will always have your back, my brother and your promise."] She answered. We continued to plow through the enemy throwing bodies aside as we strode forward. Glancing back I realized a large contingent of our men was following in our wake killing those we threw aside with the shield and making a wide path through the enemy for more to follow hacking and slashing as they came. We drew near to where the Dark Man was and there were a slew of soldiers lying grotesquely dead on the ground. The shield was gone and they were splashed with the black sludge he had thrown at them and they lay sizzling and burning in a large circle.

I raised the Black Sword and a path was made as it gently picked the dead men up and moved them aside. We barely slowed in our quest for the Dark Man as we glanced down to be sure we did not step in the black sludge as we surged forward.

The Dark Man stood on a slight rise in the ground surrounded by lightning streaming from his staff. His hat was pulled low and his red eyes pierced us from under the brim. Black hair streamed out behind him and his long leather coat filled with long rips whipped in the energy that surrounded him. He stood tall and arrogant, confident in his ability to utterly destroy me and then the world.

Violet was right overconfidence would get me killed. The Dark Man intimidated with just his presence and he knew it. I knew he was overconfident and that was going to get him killed. We spread out the five of us facing him the rest of the soldiers facing out then in alternately so we were covered both ways. The Dark Man raised his arms his staff in his right hand and we felt a drawing sensation and with a loud pop our shield was pulled from us and he absorbed it with a great show of lightning. So that's how he managed to kill all the other soldiers. The Black Sword hummed and we were all encased in individual shields that could not so easily be drawn from us since he would have to target each one of us. He had pointed his staff and slung black sludge toward us as the shields popped up. It hit the new shields and drained off us harmlessly to the ground the shield neutralized it and it turned to harmless mud. His overconfidence took a hit with that development and he took a small step back. It was probably the first time he had ever been brought up short in his bid for our world.

I dropped my shield and strode forward confident in the Black Sword to keep me safe from the sludge. Violet had my back circling and quickly killing any who slipped through the soldiers standing guard. Not one of the enemies got through her, she was my sister and she had trained well.

"So you are here little upstart with the blue eyes. Do you think those four will save you this day? That little girl doing all the killing will be fun to kill, a real challenge, is she your sister?" He asked snidely.

I strode to within five feet of him took a stand with sword raised and said, "Yes, I am here, and if you get anywhere near my sister you would be dead quicker then I am going to kill you!"

His eyes widened in surprise then narrowed in anger as he lowered his staff toward me. Black sludge shot out of it and the Black Sword started to sing a battle song as it swatted the sludge right back at the Dark Man. He stepped to the side quickly with an even more surprised look as a small ball of sludge slid down his coat with a sizzling sound. He was not immune to his own weapon. I stepped in quickly with a hard swing with the butt of the sword into his face and heard a satisfying crunch. He bent at the waist black blood pouring from his nose and I brought my leg up and caught him smack in the face again with my boot and heard another satisfying crunch this time catching his eye socket and crushing it. One of those horrendous red eyes blinked out. The Black Sword was singing in a rage wanting to bite deep into the Dark Mans flesh. I did not want him to die so easily, I wanted him to suffer as he had made so many others suffer. I wanted him to bleed and scream in pain as all those others had screamed. He swept the staff across my legs knocking them out from under me. I brought the side of the sword down across his back in a violent sweep that knocked him on his face as I hit the ground beside him. He was gasping for air in the mess that was his face as I rose to my feet. The Black Sword was singing with impatience to drink the rank blood of the Dark Man. I thought it was time also but it would be sips building up to the draft. The sword sang sweetly as it sliced down the outside right leg of the Dark Man flaying the skin aside like a filleted fish. He let out a strangled scream. It then swept up the outside left leg laying the skin out on the blood soaked ground. The Dark Man screamed again cutting it off in harsh control. The song deepened with each sip of blood as it ran back and forth across his back making small cuts that ran with blood through his coat. The Dark Man finally got his breath back and after pushing away from the ground was rising to his feet, the man had stamina or he was possessed. I believe he was possessed by the need to possess and kill, blood he wanted blood and lots of it.

He brought his staff up under my chin and the Black Sword knocked it away and he whipped it around hitting the outside of my right knee and I went down as the pain exploded in my knee. The Black Sword struck out and buried its tip in the Dark Mans thigh and he went down on one knee bringing his staff across my back as I was trying to rise, knocking me down again. I rolled away from his staff as he tried to bring it down again slicing deep into my left arm. I got stiffly to my feet favoring my right leg with blood running down my arm. The Dark Man also rose to meet me his black blood running down his legs and back. The Black Sword sang as it thirsted for the black blood of the Dark Man and it was in a rage that I bled. It was as if the sword had a life of its own pulling and surging toward the Dark Man and it was all I could do to hang on to it.

The Dark Man leaned on his staff and said, "You will die little upstart, do you think you can beat me even with that sword? That One we have not seen in so long I have forgotten when the last time was." He took a large breath and threw energy at me and the Black Sword jerked up snapping a bubble around me as the energy whipped around me trying to find a way though the shield. The Dark Man laughed as I stood there in my bubble his face swelling, one eye gone and blood dripping down his legs. The Black Sword screamed in rage and lunging forward rammed itself up to its hilt in the Dark Man chest.

He laughed and said, "You do not defeat me. Do you think I am the last? I am the least of my kind and you will die, you will all die! This world will be ours." He sank to his knees as the Black Sword pulled itself out of his chest and with one great sweep cut off his head. The head rolled to my feet its one red eye still glowing as it looked at me and laughed until the glow faded from his eye. He then melted into the earth in a puddle of black blood. I fell on my left knee, left arm hanging at my side. I leaned on the Black Sword my head bowed as I contemplated his words. He was not the last and he was the least of his kind. What did we have to look forward to? It seems we had not won the war just a battle and a feeling of great despair and hopelessness came over me. That is what he wanted, despair.

Analise, Violet, Dorian and Georges ran toward me Analise getting to me first. She poured water on a cloth lifting my chin to wash the dirt and grime away to see the bruises and the tears running down my face. Violet still had my back and stood guard.

"Where do you hurt the worst?" She asked.

I replied, "Everywhere but I don't think I can stand on my right knee or easily straighten my back and there is something wrong with my arm. But worst is my heart and soul are in despair; we did not win even though the Dark Man is dead. He was not the last and he was the least of his kind. More Dark Men will come and this world will die."

The Black Sword moved under me rising out of the ground where I had plunged it to lean upon and stay upright. It raised itself rotating in my hands to my forehead where it rested gently. Analise sat back giving me room. A warm feeling washed over me and through me glowing blue, growing hot in all the areas I was hurt. I could feel myself healing, my arm knitting together my knee and back strengthening. The energy then became cool and bubbly giving me energy and new hope. My heart was up lifted and I knew I must not despair as hopelessness fell from me. I lift my head up knowing we could and must prevail in this war that was not over yet. The Black Sword was here for me, would energize me when I faltered, hold me up when I stumbled and fight beside me to victory. I rose to my feet energized looking at my companions. I knew this physical world may die but the world of mankind would live. We will live! Fight for the light, live in the light!

CHAPTER TWENTY-THREE

I then looked around realizing the fighting had stopped. The Dark Man had fallen and the poor souls under his power were lying in the blood and mud weeping. Our soldiers stood gazing upon them some in anger others in confusion not knowing what to do. Others were bending down offering assistance and compassion. They remembered what we saw in the last village and what these poor souls were forced to do to those they loved.

I bowed my head a moment then said, "We must burn the enemy dead. Our dead must be transported back to their Kingdoms. Georges please set a detail to go to the castle and request cloth or materials for shrouds for the dead. We will show them respect as they are taken home to rest. Dorian please set a detail to pile the enemy dead as far from the castle as is appropriate, several piles will be needed. We will set them afire from a distance once it is accomplished. Analise could you get some people looking after the wounded?"

Not as many of our soldiers had died as I feared, the shield had kept many safe. We still placed too many in lines sorting them by Kingdom so they could go home to their people for burial. We had thirteen to take back to Castle Clarion other Kingdoms had more some less but they all went home. We were done sorting the dead and had set the piles of enemy on fire making an oily light. We gathered the weeping enemy soldiers together.

The gates of Castle Laird had opened and people poured out. Men carrying great cauldrons of a thick stew, women carrying baskets of fresh bread, rolls and cheese cut in hunks. Barrels of mead were rolled out and cups provided as well as bowls and spoons. The men though they were finishing disheartening work needed to eat and it was a welcome sight. More women came some with cloth, thread and needle and some with bandages, splints and salves. Others came with pails of soapy water and rags; they knelt before our dead washing them, cleaning and straightening their clothes. They sewed them into shrouds with a flap covering their faces so they could be seen one last time by their loved ones. They helped bandage the wounded making them comfortable until we could get them home. The King had taken responsibility for the weeping men that were left of the Dark Mans army. Many had killed themselves when they came to their senses when the Dark Man fell, falling upon their swords.

When all the good deeds were done, and the soldiers fed I raised the Black Sword. It started to sing as I opened doors into the Kingdoms we had come from. The wounded were picked up and carried or helped through the doors. Friends and companions bore their dead upon their shoulders taking them home one last time their heads held up in pride, they had fought well.

King Laird of Castle Laird came forward to talk to me as the last door closed but ours into Clarion.

He asked, "What of the Dark Man? Is it over?"

I looked him straight in the eye and said, "I killed the Dark Man but it is not over. There are more Dark Men coming and he was the least of their kind."

"I feared it was not over. He was the least, heh?" He said.

I replied, "Yes."

"We must prepare to meet them; do you know when another will come?" He asked.

"No I don't, but we must act quickly and prepare everyone as if it is tomorrow for it may be." I said. "We have the Black Sword so take heart; it will lead us to Victory against whatever they send at us."

As our dead were gathered up by their friends to be transported home the Black Sword began to sing. As the last person stepped through the door the Sword pointed itself toward Castle Laird and a blue fire flared from its tip. The symbol of the Black Sword, the same that was burned onto my chest was burned into the wall next to the door.

I looked at the King of Laird and said, "Remember! Come when the Black Sword sings!

I stepped toward the door where Analise, Violet, Dorian and Georges waited for me. He said with a bow, "I thank you, bearer of the Black Sword for my Kingdom and our freedom. We will come when you call."

He nodded as only Kings can nod and I nodded back. I stepped through the door into the meadow below Castle Clarion and the door snapped shut. We followed the procession of dead with the wounded and hale soldiers, my four friends by my side as we walked up and into the castle.

There were cries and grieving for the dead as there always has been and always will be for the loss of loved ones and concern for the wounded. I walked slowly though the gathered people giving comfort where I could. Grieving with our people was akin to grieving for my own family lost so long ago. I knew I could not let myself grieve until I went home one last time. As I withdrew from the crowd of people in the Great Room Violet found me against the wall.

["We must travel to the mountains."] She said.

["I fear things may go bad if we leave."] I protested.

["But we must."] She said.

["Yes, after the Black Sword sings the souls of our people to the stars and before it all starts again, you're right we must go."] I replied.

Violet nodded and walked away. The dead soldiers would have a night and a day with those who loved them. The pyres were to be prepared for the next sundown. I sighed; there was nothing else I could do here so I headed back to my room. There was a hot bath drawn and clean towels lay out. I still don't know how they know when to draw a bath or how they get the towels so fluffy, I thought fingering a towel. I lay the Black Sword on the bed and dropped my filthy bloody clothes in a pile. I had left what little armor I wore in the Great Room. I sank into a tub of hot water submerging until I could no longer hold my breath then bursting from the water. Dorian was leaning against the bathroom door frame. I wiped the water from my face and poured hair soap into the palm of my hand then rubbed it into my hair.

"I understand you are taking a trip to the mountains." Dorian stated.

I stopped in mid scrub, "How do you know that?" I asked.

"Its obvious, big fight, people die, you and Violet, grieving, closure. You need to go home and work it out before we are deep in trouble again." He said.

"We need to go alone." I said, continuing to wash my hair.

"Bad idea." He said. "Best place to remove you two; we need you both to much to risk losing you."

I paused looking at him and asked, "Are you really that worried about it? I'll have the Black Sword with me and Violet is an Assassin."

"You will also have the ghosts of your family." He said. "Believe me when I say I know how hard it is to deal with that. You will be in no shape to watch your back."

"Have you talked to Violet?" I asked.

"No, I came to you. I figured you would be……… easier to reason with." He said.

I laughed and said, "I'll bet you did. You have made some good points. I'll talk to Violet. Who are you thinking should go with us?"

"After we button down the castle, set guards, contact the other Kingdoms and work out an alarm we can hear. All five of us go." He said. "It will be like a vacation for us before the storm hits."

I went under to rinse my hair, coming up I said, "Some vacation. OK, I'm up for it. At daybreak, after the memorial for our fallen soldiers, we meet in the Great Room. We'll be camping, of course you know that better then me having seen the devastation to our home." I dumped more soap in my hand and began washing my body.

"Thank you Trevor for being so open minded. I really don't know what the Kingdoms would do without either of you at this time. You need to be safe guarded for all our sakes. I grieved for your family long ago. Under your circumstances we all respect your need to grieve for your sisters and parents at this time. I will make an excellent guard. And there is body soap." Dorian said, then turned and left locking the door behind him.

I thought about what he said and knew he was right. Violet and I had no right to be taking off on a jaunt by ourselves with so much at stake. It would be nice to have our friends there and Dorian might be able to answer any questions we might have. I knocked on the door in Violets head and related my and Dorian's conversation and the conclusions I had come to, surprisingly she agreed.

I finished washing after trying the body soap, got out of the tub and reached for a towel. It was soft and fluffy, how did they do that? I dried myself and quickly shaved, I was getting good at it. I went into my bedroom noticing my dirty clothes were gone, I didn't know how they did that either. I checked myself over and found not a scratch anywhere. I looked with appreciation at the Black Sword, who had healed me, realizing it was clean and oiled and I didn't know how that happened either. I was suddenly overwhelmed with exhaustion so I crawled into bed beneath the covers and fell instantly asleep. It had been a long horrible and grueling day.

CHAPTER TWENTY-FOUR

I woke slowly the next morning and lay there looking around my room. This was the first morning someone had not knocked on my door bringing me clean clothes and urging me to hurry. It felt strange. A somber gray was filtering through the cracks in the drapes over my windows so I knew it was still early. Being an early riser I got up rinsed my face, cleaned my teeth, brushed and pulled back my hair. I then went to the closet looking for clothes I could pick out myself since none were laid out for me. I opened the closet and was surprised at the number of clothes hanging there. I picked out a deep blue silk shirt and pants of black leather. I pulled them on and my stomach rumbled. I pulled on my soft boots and headed out to the War Room where I knew I could get some breakfast.

The castle was quiet as I walked through the hallways. I was not in a hurry so I could enjoy and appreciate the paintings on the walls, the tapestries and small tables with art objects sitting on them. It was a pleasant stroll when you're not in a hurry as I am sure it was meant to be. I came to the end of the hall where it turned left and there before me hung a large painting of a garden filled with the most beautiful flowers growing against a mountain with the bluest skies above it. Set in the mountain was a golden door carved with trees, flowers and birds with a large golden handle. It was the door in Analise's head. To the right of the door was a small girl picking flowers and putting them in a basket. I knew that garden and door were real somewhere and that little girl was Analise. It was a breath taking painting and I wondered that I had not noticed it before. I had another mystery; where is that garden? I stood drinking the beauty of it in for a few more minutes when my stomach growled loud enough to get my attention. Reluctantly I turned and walked on to find some breakfast thinking I would look at the painting again at a later time.

I looked in the War Room and it was empty so I peeked in the kitchen and found a bustle of activity. Cook noticed me and shoeing me out motioned for the servers to start dishing up food. I went back to the War Room followed shortly by servers and a steady flow of food. They brought hot black coffee, sweetener and cream, pitchers of milk, hot sweet rolls with slabs of butter melting on them, scrambled, poached or fried eggs with rashers of bacon and slabs of ham with three different kinds of potatoes. I grabbed a hot plate and started filling it noticing a bowl of berries, where did they get berries this time of year? I filled my plate and dug in eating with gusto it was so good. I was filling my plate a second time and making a dent in the food when Dorian and Georges walked in. I nodded and mumbled good morning with my mouth full of sweet roll. They grabbed plates filling them as I had and sat down to eat. I was slowing down when they got up for seconds. I leaned back sipping coffee with generous helpings of cream and sweetener and nibbling my third sweet roll. I looked at Dorian and Georges noticing small bruises and scratches from the battle yesterday. They seemed stiff with fatigue and muscle aches as though the rest over night had not treated them well. I felt a pang of guilt that I felt so well since the Black Sword had healed me. I wondered how much healing it could do and decided to find out before we left for the mountains in the morning. It wouldn't do to have everyone stiff and sore.

Dorian finished his second plate and leaned back with a sweet roll and a large cup of coffee hot and black. He said, "We have details building funeral pyres, thirteen on the meadow outside the Postern gate. They will be ready by nightfall. We need to meet with the Water Guard who is doing an excellent job, let them know how long we will be gone and to be extra alert. All the captains are on alert to be summoned here; we should pick a good man to leave in charge so there is no confusion if there is a problem. After lunch we will contact the Kingdoms, and we need to figure out how we can be alerted if there is a problem."

I took a sip of coffee and asked, "Do you know of anyone in the castle who can channel besides Analise, Violet and me? That would be the best way to call us."

Dorian shook his head no as Analise and Violet walked in. They both picked up plates and filled them with food poured cups of coffee and came to sit down. Violet took a sip of her sweetened coffee and a bite of egg.

She said, "Have you opened your door lately?"

Immediately interested I said, "No I haven't what's up?"

She smiled and said, "Give it a crack and be ready to slam it shut."

Concerned I did what she asked and heard a soft babble then, ["mik, mik, mor, mor,"] and a screech when what I figured to be milk didn't come as fast as wanted and I slammed my door shut.

"Oh my god, Hope can channel. She's only what eighteen months or so? She can channel already?" I asked.

Violet and Analise both smiled and Analise answered, "Rude awakening huh! She of course can't control it and everything comes through, but our little prodigy can channel. She is very loud."

I slowly opened my door and I suddenly winced as a screech filled my head and I heard a, ["There, there its Ok here's your bottle darlin."] Then a happy gurgle and sucking sounds and I slowly closed it as I sat thinking.

"I can hear Jasmine talking to her." I said.

Violet and Analise both said, "Really!"

We all opened our doors and sat listening to Jasmine patter to Hope and Hope giggling when she tickled her when she seemed to be changing her. Here is our communication I thought, Jasmine could talk to us through Hope. How much do eighteen month olds sleep anyway? I couldn't remember.

I said, ["Hi Hope this is Uncle Trevor, how was your milk honey?']

Hope babbled, ["Mik, mik, mmmmm, cookie?"]

She had heard me and answered as best as she could and she wanted a cookie. I would have to bring her one later. I looked at Analise and Violet and we closed our doors.

I looked at Dorian and said, "We have our communication, anyway when she's awake.

Dorian laughed and said, "We are going to depend on an eighteen month old to let us know if something goes wrong?"

"No," I said, "I can hear Jasmine talking to Hope so she can let us know through Hope. We just have to have our doors open. We'll have to take turns, baby babble can be wearing."

Dorian looked at me seriously and said, "Is that normal to hear other people through a mind door?"

"I don't know. It is a rare thing to be telepathic and it usually doesn't develop until a child is older. My first experience was when Analise called me when I was twelve. How old were you Violet?" I asked, and then I remembered she had heard our family die when she was two.

I put my hand on her shoulder and said. "I'm sorry Violet, I wasn't thinking."

Violet said, "Obviously stress brings out the ability at any age, I was two, Hope eighteen months. We both underwent a lot of stress at those ages. The norm is probably between eight and twelve." Analise agreed.

Analise and Violet finished breakfast and were going to visit Jasmine and Hope to explain to Jasmine how she could help us. I had them take cookies to Hope for me since I was going to be busy for a while. I planned on seeing them before we left in the morning.

The day wore on as we talked to the Water Guard. Captain Jondar taking our leaving seriously asked for more soldiers to watch the water supply. When we met with the Captains we appointed Captain Lee Reed to Major Captain in our absence. Georges knew him personally and vouched for him as an excellent choice to lead the men while we were gone. Dorian had agreed though he didn't know him personally he knew his reputation and it was all good. The Castle Guard was alerted and extra men assigned, I was not going to leave and leave Castle Clarion vulnerable. It would be protected to the maximum.

We were having lunch in the War Room, a hot thick stew, fresh bread cut in great slabs with fresh butter, cold cuts, fruits and asparagus. Pitchers of ale were available as well as coffee and water. Analise and Violet were both lunching with Jasmine and Hope to continue working out our communication piece. Jasmine was truly surprised we could hear her through Hope. She thought it was kind of creepy but useful and agreed to help keep us informed on events inside the castle. I finished my stew and was eating a ham sandwich thinking about the painting I had seen in the hallway.

I looked at Dorian and asked, "Where is the garden in the painting at the end of the hall where my bedroom is?"

His hand stopped half way to his mouth with a spoonful of stew. Surprised he asked, "You saw the painting, a garden with the golden door?"

Puzzled, I said, "Yes, and I was wondering where such a beautiful place could be and thought you would know. The little girl is obviously Analise and she looks so happy picking flowers. It must be a real place it looks so real. Do you know where it is?"

Dorian had put his spoon down and he said, "You saw a little girl who you believe to be Analise, picking flowers in the painting?"

"If it isn't her then whoever it is looks just like her." I said. "Why, isn't it her?"

He thought a moment, sighed and said, "Not everyone sees that painting. Everyone who has seen it sees the golden door in the garden; you are the first that I know of to see a girl, any girl, picking flowers or not. You say the girl looked like Analise?"

I put my sandwich down and said, "What?"

"The painting," Dorian explained, "Is not seen by everyone, very few actually. They are usually members of the Clarion family and it has special meaning for each of them. I have never seen it though it has been described, so I vaguely know what it looks like. I am told the door is painted in actual gold and it is beyond beautiful. When did you see it and what did you see?"

I was totally surprised and unprepared for what he told me. How could I have seen such a painting? I know I did but how did I? I sat back in my chair and looked at Dorian, maybe he was pulling my leg, no, he was definitely not kidding around. He was way too serious to be joking.

I stammered, "How did I see it?"

He said, "I don't know. What did you see?"

I described the painting, the abundant flower garden full of color at the base of a mountain. I told him about the golden door inset in the mountain and carved with trees, flowers and birds, which by the way was also the door in Analise's head. I went on to describe the skies that were such a pure blue it looked like the actual sky was brought in and laid on the canvas. I finally said there was a beautiful little girl with long red curls tumbling down her back and green eyes flecked in gold. She was wearing a long white dress bending over picking flowers and putting them into a basket that sat on the ground. She looked right at me with those eyes that could only be Analise's. She was putting a flower up to her nose to smell, had a secretive smile on her lips and a twinkle in her eyes. She must have been about nine but it was Analise.

"My god, I have never heard such a description of the painting, the girl sounds just like Analise. There has never been a girl in the painting." He said.

Analise spoke up, "There has been since I was nine. It was hanging in the nursery. It was the only time I have ever seen it and I loved it. Before that it was the garden and the door."

We turned and Analise was standing behind us her face white, her hands clutched over her breast.

"You really saw it Trevor, didn't you? You must have, I heard you describe it as no one has ever described it." Analise said as she slowly sat down.

I looked at her and asked, "What does it mean? You really have never seen it again?"

She said, "I have not seen it since the day I turned nine and I loved it ever since and I have looked for it everywhere. That was the year I was moved to my own rooms. It has appeared to others only once maybe twice with me in it. It has been seen three maybe four times and I'm not in it. It is not seen often. I don't know what it means, but I would like to find out. Could you let me know if you see it again?"

"Of course I will, I'll show it to you if I see it again. Someone must know what it means; maybe we can find who painted it and what it means." I said.

She bowed her head and said, "If only it was that easy. That painting has been in this castle for generations. It has moved and disappeared sometimes for years but I am the first person to ever be seen in it. Some of the servants think the painting haunts the castle, showing up out of the blue in different places. I just don't know why I'm in it now, or what it means."

Georges interrupted us saying, "While this is all fascinating and I want to know what is going on as much as you do. We need to contact the other Kingdoms before nightfall so we can give the dead their memorial.

$$ \text{———} \maltese \text{———} $$

CHAPTER TWENTY-FIVE

Dorian looked at all of us and said, "He is right we need to move ahead. Analise, when we get back from the mountains we will delve into this more. There has to be a reason Trevor saw the painting with you in it and we will find out the reason."

Analise agreed it was of utmost importance to talk to the Kings as Violet walked into the room. She immediately sensed something was off and asked what was going on. Georges told her something extremely interesting had happened but less important at this time then contacting the other Kingdoms. He said he would inform her later and she nodded.

We all gathered on one side of a long table and Violet and I opened doors into the Great Rooms of the other Kingdoms. Most times the King was present, sometimes a runner was sent to bring him to us. They were all preparing for further invasion. We told them to watch for something different or out of sorts. They may not come back using the same tactics and that made many pause and think. We explained we would be away for a few days but would be in constant contact with Castle Clarion. We did not tell them our contact was an eighteen month old baby. It took all afternoon but we were finally done.

We all felt that except for the casualties, fighting a war was easier then sitting and talking to diplomats all day. We had time for a quick meal just before the sun set. Food was brought into the War Room, roast chicken and roasted potatoes with clotted cream and new peas. A different type of roll that was light and fluffy with butter and jams and fruit pies. We had the usual ale though a bit darker, water or milk and as usual it was all delicious.

Georges informed Violet while we ate what we had discussed before she got here. She was alarmed by a ghost painting haunting the castle and is sure it means something we need to know about. But she realized we would have to wait till we got back to solve the mystery.

The sun was setting as we finished and we all rose putting on our outer gear. We made our way to the Postern Gate where the soldiers in their shrouds were being carried out followed by their families. They were placed upon the thirteen pyres set in a circle amid wailing and weeping. War is a horror and a burden; parents should not outlive their children which happens all too often in war.

I walked to the center of the thirteen pyres as I had before and wondered how many more times I would have to do this before we knew peace.

I drew the Black Sword and bowed my head over it as if in prayer. I asked it to give me the words to relieve and mend these people's hearts.

I lifted my head and said, "I want to say you must be proud. I want to say you should be joyous. But how, when your child is dead, your son, daughter, husband, lover, life, hope, is dead. Why joyous? Because they were more then your son, daughter, husband, lover. They were Soldiers. Yes they were life, yes they were hope and yes they loved you, always remember that, because you are who they were fighting for when they died. You represent freedom, freedom from the machinations of the Dark Man. Freedom to live far from the slow death the Dark Man offers. Freedom to love, live and hope; that's what they fought for. That's what they gave their lives for. As long as you live they live in you. Be proud. Make their death count, make it important and live, love, laugh, and be free. Be free!"

The Black Sword began to sing as the pyres were lit and its energy entwined with the smoke from the fires. It ushered the souls of the soldiers up to the stars. It sang in triumph, sorrow and joy. The pure beauty of the song brought people to their knees and families together. In the end it wrote the names of the dead upon the Postern Gate wall to join the names of all those fallen in the name of freedom.

The fires died down and we filed into the castle and to our beds. The ashes would be collected in the morning and distributed to the families. It was early to rise for the five of us. For the families it was learning to rise with a hole in their lives. That was exactly why we were going to the mountains in the morning, the holes in our lives, mine and Violets needed mending.

As soon as I reached my room I took off my clothes dropping them in a pile as I headed to the bath to wash the stench of smoke from the pyres. I smelled too much like death to sleep as I was. The bath was drawn and hot with plenty of fluffy towels. How did they do that? I climbed in and submerged until I could no longer hold my breath, emerging from the water I began to scrub. My hair, my body, my hair again, I don't know what I was trying to scrub away. The memory of tonight or the memory of the past I was about to encounter. The death of my parents and three of my sisters in a massacre Violet saw and lived through to become the Assassin she was. God how could I tell those people to be joyous, death was not joyous. It was lonely wasn't it? My parents gained what? Life for me and Violet, did they believe it was worth it? Yes, they gave their lives as sacrifice for Violet and me. They must have thought it was worth it or why would they do it? I climbed out of the tub dried off and looked in the mirror and thought, to hell with shaving. I'm going camping; you don't shave when you go camping. I'd just get a head start and not shave. I fell into bed and into a deep sleep where only my demons walk and burn me with the guilt that I was alive and my family was not.

I rose early as usual. It was another day when no one was banging on my door. I pulled the drapes back to see a gray but cloudless sky. After rinsing my face, cleaning my teeth and pulling back my hair I dressed for the mountains in thick heavy pants and a blue wool shirt with an under shirt. I pulled on heavy wool socks before I pulled on the boots given to me by Georges brother. I don't know how the clothes get in my closet but I always had what I need. There was a hip length leather coat made for hiking and ease of movement that I pulled out as well as heavy leather gloves and a wool hat the color of my eyes.

I picked up my pack looking at it. All my original stuff was still on it so I packed a change of clothes and several pair of wool socks, it's important to have extra socks. I would pick up some food to carry in the kitchen. I was sure we would be bringing plenty of food. I like to be prepared for anything so I always carried my own traveling food such as jerky, dried fruit and hard tack along with bottles of water. It didn't taste great but would keep me alive if needed. My gun was packed in the bottom of my pack; guns were unusual but could be handy if attacked and some things only die by metal. I thought about the one hundred forty-nine dollars I had kept in my boot. I probably never would have found a rifle if I had ever saved enough. I realized dad had never discouraged a dream. I sat down on the bed letting it sink in; our parents had done everything for us by letting us believe in ourselves, letting us dream even if reality was different from the dream. That was why we could do the things we could do. We were not inhibited by preconceived notions put in our heads by insecure people. Our parents had let us be free thinkers thus setting us free. That's why we could simply accept the new things we could do, we were free to do so. I bowed my head thinking about the insights into my parent's skills as parents. They were selfless free thinkers and they passed it to us with generous helpings of pure love. I felt a great sadness that they were gone and I could not let them know how much their sacrifices and love had helped me to simply be me. To be able to accept things in myself other people would not be able to accept in themselves.

There was a knock on my door interrupting my thoughts. I went to answer the door and there stood Dorian.

I grinned and said, "This is becoming a habit."

He rolled his eyes and said, "Violet sent me, and she told me you were lost in thoughts and needed to be prodded or it would be noon before we got started."

I looked at the drapes and could see the sun peeking through.

"How did it get so late, what time is it anyway?" I asked.

"The sun just slipped over the mountain so it is not very late. We must be going and you need to breakfast and visit Jasmine and Hope before we can leave." He replied.

"I am ready to go," I said turning to get my pack, coat, gloves and hats. I stuffed the blue knit hat into my bag with my gloves and put my leather hat on. I picked up the Black Sword tucking it under my arm after slinging my pack on my shoulder. I would put the sword on after I ate and saw Jasmine and Hope. We went out closing the door.

We walked to the War room where breakfast was laid out for us. Today it was pancakes, great piles of plain, blueberry, and some kind of nut. Great dollops of butter topped them with generous portions of syrup. Platters of Ham and bacon, scrambled eggs and fruit as well as coffee and juice were all on the side board waiting for us. Georges gave a slight wave sitting in front of an empty plate with a cup of coffee. I was surprised to see Jasmine and Hope sitting at the table, each with a generous portion in front of them. Hope was sitting in a little booster seat I had never seen before and she was dribbling syrup down her chin. She had a kitchen towel tucked under her chin to protect her clothes. She looked so cute sitting at the big table. She looked up at me from her pile of mangled pancakes and I noticed how blue her eyes were. They were a true sapphire that sparkled with mirth.

She smiled a pancake smile and yelled, "Unca Rev, unca Rev, cake, cake." Waving her fork around she was so excited to have pancakes and I realized to see me. I put my pack, coat and sword down against the wall and went to sit by her. She wacked me in the arm with her fork and pointing at the food she yelled, "Cake,

cake." Grinning I got up and filled a plate then came back and sat next to her.

"How's this?" I asked. Hope nodded and shoved another piece of pancake into her mouth. I took a big bite of mine and realized why she was so excited they were really good. I chewed my food relishing each bite. I looked at Jasmine on the other side of Hope she had a huge smile on her face.

I swallowed and said, "Hope has good taste in pancakes."

She said, "Hope has good taste in everything. I haven't found a food yet she won't eat."

Hope said, "Eat, eat." She waved her fork around in the air. We all laughed including Violet and Analise who had just walked in.

Analise said, "It looks like you're all having fun."

Analise and Violet both filled plates and sat to eat. That made Hope happy, it seemed important to her that everyone eat. We finished our breakfast and Hope got down. She wanted to go around the table and visit with everyone. We sat back to finish our coffee as I observed Jasmine and how she watched her little charge. She seemed genuinely fond of Hope and that made me feel good about her in the role of nanny for the blue eyed child.

I cleared my throat a bit to get Jasmines attention then said, "Analise and Violet have been working with you communicating telepathically through Hope. How do you feel about it? Are you ready to be our only communication with the castle?"

"You get right to the point don't you?" Jasmine asked.

"I don't have time to do it any other way." I replied.

"Well, it was scary at first because I could hear them in my head the way I can hear Hope babble. I am not telepathic at all or so I thought. I have never heard anyone else. I've gotten used to it though and it's not so creepy having someone in my head." She said, looking at her coffee.

I opened the Red Door in my head and asked telepathically. ["You are ready to be communication officer now that you are comfortable with telepathy?"]

Still looking at her coffee she said, "Yes I think I am. I just don't know how I would react to you being in my head. Can you access any other part of my brain?"

["No we can't access any part of the brain except the communication center. Your personal thoughts and memories are safe in your head. You seem to be a receiver and cannot transmit unless you have a link to work through like Hope. As far as worrying about how it will be with me talking in your head, this conversation has been spoken telepathically. I have been talking in your head."]

Her head whipped around and she looked at me startled. She said, "You didn't warn me!"

I smiled and said, ["I wanted to see how comfortable you are with it and you did wonderful. What did you think Hope?"]

Hope giggled and said, ["Unca Rev funny, funny."]

I chased after her amidst shrieks of laughter and tickled her giving Jasmine time to recover. I finally sat down next to Jasmine and smiled at her.

"I believe you are ready. I am confident we can leave you in charge as communications officer. If anything goes wrong here I know you can alert us and we can return. You have also done wonders with little Hope. She seems to have no ill affects from her ordeal." I said.

She looked at Hope who was laying and yawning on my lap and smiled fondly.

"She is a joy to take care of. I hope she never has ill affects; she still could even though she was drugged but I hope not. I also think she is older then she presents herself but that could be effects from the drugs. She is too sweet to be troubled by an ugly past. I really appreciate your confidence in me. Hope and I will do our very best as communication officers to keep you all informed while you are absent. Won't we Hope?" She said.

Hope yawned and nodded her head. Jasmine got up and said, "I better take her to her room for a short nap. She was up running around early and she still seems to need a morning nap. I'm sure she will grow out of it quick enough." She picked Hope up out of my lap. "We have worked out a schedule to communicate when Hope is awake so I will be talking to you soon." She gathered up the sleepy little girl, nodded to Analise and Violet leaving the room with Hope giving a sleepy wave.

CHAPTER TWENTY-SIX

We all looked at each other then Violet said, "Way to go Bro, she was nervous about talking to you telepathically and you just gave her a huge boost of confidence. I'm sure there will be no problems with communication while we are gone."

"We need to be gone," Dorian said.

We all stood up as cook came in with packages of traveling food for our packs. We all had enough food for several days and considering the time of year there should be game in the mountains. Fresh meat on a camping trip was always a treat. We put them in our bags, thanking cook. She said there would be a special meal in three days to welcome our return. We thanked her some more saying we would look forward to it.

The five of us trooped out of the castle to the meadow below. I knew I could block a return so no one could follow it back coming out into the castle, but why chance it when we were leaving.

"I am going to open a door to Devils Deep, a lake we used to swim in when we were kids. It's about three miles from the house and there used to be a good trail. It was an animal trail so some remnant should still be there. If not I can still find my way.

Dorian said, "I remember the lake and the trail. That lake is colder then the Devils heart."

I laughed, "You have swum in it! That's why we were never good swimmers, it's to cold to stay in and practice.

I closed my eyes and visualized the lake, and then I opened the door on the edge. We glanced back and saw the ramparts were full of people watching us leave. We could hear the gasps of those who could see through the door and the lake surrounded by mountains in it. We all lifted a hand to the people and they waved back as we stepped through and the door winked shut.

We stood on the edge of a large dark lake in the midst of a heavy forest of evergreens. Snow capped mountains rose up around us. We were in the bowl of a large mountain valley where the lake and our childhood home were located. Violet looked around her eyes wide with recognition.

"I feel this place." She said, "I have a vague visual but my feelings for this place are strong.

I took her hand in mine and projected a memory of a picnic our family had here when we were little into her mind. I wanted her to have some happy memories of our home, as I did.

Mom was laying out a picnic on a blue blanket with a black stripe. There was a large pile of sandwiches probably chicken salad her favorite. A bunch of vegetables were in bowls cut and ready to eat. The best part was the chocolate cake. We didn't get cake very often and chocolate was our entire family's favorite.

Violet was on the blanket with mom chewing on a carrot looking adorable in a blue romper. Lily and I were out in the water practicing swimming when we weren't splashing each other. Dad had Rose in the water instructing her on how to swim. Daisy was on the shore shivering in her green polka dotted swim suit waiting her turn in the water.

A big pile of towels were heaped on the shore so when we got out we could immediately wrap up. They were the stiff line dried variety. It was a beautiful peaceful day. Dad sent Rose to shore and called Daisy who stepped gingerly into the water then boldly dove in surfacing next to dad. Dad smiled fondly at her and started to teach Daisy how to swim. Mom called and we all looked her way. She waved us in for lunch. We all scrambled out of the water grabbing towels to dry ourselves and warm us up. We all sat around on the blanket eating sandwiches and munching veggies. When we had eaten enough we all got a piece of chocolate cake. We all slowed down except Violet, she crammed that cake in her mouth. She chewed and smiled and licked her hands as the rest of us nibbled and gently licked the frosting to make it last as long as possible. Dad told a joke and we all laughed and I let the memory fade.

Violet opened her eyes and I could see tears glinting in them. She looked at me and said, "Thank you Trevor. That was a sweet memory."

"I didn't think you had enough happy memories of this place since you were so young when you left." I said.

It had only taken a few minutes but Dorian, Georges and Analise had drifted to the shore to give us a few minutes of privacy. Dorian was watching the woods intently. Analise looked over the lake and Georges was skipping stones of all things. It looked like fun. I looked at Violet and asked her if she could skip stones.

Violet said, "We didn't learn about killing people all the time." She ran to the shore yelling, "A point for every skip and the most points wins."

She didn't say what we would win but I was up for the game. Dorian let us play for an hour then gently urged us to move on down the trail. We needed to set up camp before nightfall and we had three miles to hike. Georges had won, and we were all laughing when we picked up our packs and I located the trail. We began hiking and I was surprised at how well the trail was maintained by the animals that used it. It was peaceful walking under the branches of towering pine trees. The birds chattered and the song birds sang sweet tunes in the trees. Butterflies flitted among the lower branches and we saw a doe and fawn through the trees standing in a ray of sunshine. Shade flowers dotted the under growth in bright colors. There was a gentle breeze whispering through the needles on the trees causing them to gently shimmer. It was beautiful. Analise was looking all around with wide eyes drinking in the beauty as if the bubble might pop any minute and it all disappear. Violet was doing the same only more intently as if she was trying to find something or see something she would recognize.

It was as familiar to me as if I had hiked this trail yesterday. Dorian was ahead of us as lead lookout and Georges was behind watching our backs. I did not expect trouble but that was usually when it found me. What I didn't remember was how beautiful the forest was. The peace of the quiet though it was not truly quiet with the song and rustling of the wind. The way the sun shot through the trees making golden shafts of light. Shafts that slanted down into pools of gold that small animals and birds played in and deer lay dozing in the warmth amid the cool shade. I walked and I marveled that as a child I did not notice or appreciate the place where I grew up. I knocked on Violets door and she opened to such wonder it took my breath away.

I asked, ["Do you remember any of this beauty when we were children?"]

["I remember the feeling, like the Great Hall in the Palace of Assassins. Quiet majesty and domination without fear a quiet determination to be felt and awed."] She replied.

We left our doors open so we could feel or discuss what we were seeing. We heard a small brook babbling that was hidden at first though when we heard it we both remembered it. It came into view when the trail turned around a large tree and there it was falling into a series of pools. Dragonflies flitted over the pools and water spiders skimmed the water. Violet shivered, she had never liked the water spiders but she liked watching the minnows that swam in the pools. We walked over and she was glad they were still there as if they were the same ones. I worried she was reverting to times past when she said she knew when she was, it was just nice to glimpse the past and remember the good stuff.

We hiked on and I knew we were coming closer to the homestead where I was a child and she just a baby. Violet felt she had never been a baby. The forest started to thin where we had cut trees for firewood it made more open spaces where young deciduous trees were coming up that were easier for the deer to browse.

I saw a lot of deer pellets and pointed them out so we knew they had moved in. I was glad that there were living things still here and Violet agreed. It did not feel so abandoned with so many wholesome creatures living and playing in our wood as we used to.

Chapter Twenty-Seven

Then there it was; the clearing where our home had stood. It opened up suddenly when we walked around a large tree. It took us by surprise and we both stood with mouths agap. The out buildings still stood though in disrepair. The house is what astonished us the most. As it had burned the logs fell in and around putting the fire out themselves. The interior was gone but the outline of the house was still there with the fallen logs. A large tree with spreading branches rose high from the center. Its leaves were large and vibrant green and there were white flowers that hung from the branches in great clusters. The aroma was incredible, making our mouths water. It looked like the tree was fenced in by the logs outlining the house. We both wondered how such a beautiful tree could grow so big so fast and what kind of tree was it.

We looked further and saw four flower gardens outlined with logs, Lilies, Roses, Daisies, and Violets. I could feel Violets heart give a little lurch when she recognized the small gardens our mother had planted at the birth of each girl. She whispered in my head that she thought she had made it up when she was little to comfort herself but the memory was true. There really were flower beds for each of the girls. I nodded as tears ran down my face. I could not speak. I did not know this little thing that still remained could be my undoing. I walked over to the blooming beds fell to my knees and cried for my beautiful sisters, all of them. I felt such gut wrenching sadness and we had just got here. Violet stood by my side comforting me by her very presence though she shed not a tear. I wept enough for both of us.

I was finally able to pull myself together. I got up to carefully look at each bed and to smell each flower. Bringing back memories of each girl, memories I shared with Violet, even ones of herself because she had lost them.

We looked around and could not see our companions but we could hear them. Searching we found them in the clearing behind the old wood shed where we used to cut wood. There was still wood stacked probably wood I myself had chopped. They were making camp here where the wood was close and a small stream was not far away for water. It was also out of sight of the house and yard to afford us some privacy when we were there. It also gave us a break from thinking constantly about what happened, an out of sight out of mind sort of thing. The entire area was also easy to watch and guard unless entirely overrun. My father was a smart man he knew where to build for greatest protection.

We both sat down by the fire closing our doors by mutual agreement. We had enough memories and emotions for a while we needed to regroup ourselves.

I asked Dorian, "Where did the tree come from that is growing in the house and who planted it?

He said, "The Palace of the Assassins." Violet looked up sharply and he then related the story as he built a fire and stared to prepare food for a late lunch.

Word had come quickly though not quick enough to the outside world that the Blue Eyes in the northern mountains were being attacked. The Dawson family needed our aid. Word came by a pigeon that flew into the Palace early one morning. He pointed at the decaying pigeon cote and asked if we remembered the pigeons. We both remembered feeding and playing with the pigeons we thought were dad's pets, he liked birds.

My brother contacted me from the Palace. We gathered people and arms ready to fight and stepped through a door into a massacre. Your family was dead and they left no one for us to fight. The few attackers that were alive had gone leaving their dead, there were too many to take with them or dispose of.

Teague, your father knew they were coming. He was a precog and had sent the pigeon to warn us before they came. He could not always see things clearly or know precisely when something would happen. When our own death is involved things get even more muddled and they came quicker then he expected. He and the girls were prepared; they were always prepared and ready to defend themselves and their home. But this was the day enemies of truth came to wipe blue eyes off the face of the earth.

You had been gone five months Trevor. Teague had bows, arrows, swords and knives hidden all over the homestead. He had seen his own death but he hoped that the girls would escape. Your mother Tessa knew it was not to be but let the hope live so they would not become disheartened and would stay vigilant. Wherever anyone was on the homestead they could be armed within seconds. He taught the girls to wear knives hidden in their clothes, and he forbid dresses. Pants were easier to move and fight in, he knew a fight was coming and he would not leave his girls defenseless. They planned and made a place to hide Violet then he wiped it from their minds so they could not reveal it if tortured. He knew Violet had to survive or the world would not survive just as you had to survive Trevor. Tessa was beside him the entire time teaching and exhorting them to hone their fighting skills. They would practice. He would hide Violet teaching her to lie still and make no noise and the girls were trained not to call or look for her. No one must know she existed, they learned to accept that she was gone and they did not know where.

The food was done and I held up my hand for him to stop.

"Why did he send me away? I left following a voice but I know he put me on the Island of Dreams. If I had been here things could have been different, I could have saved them." I said in controlled frustration.

I could see the pity in Dorian's eyes, he simply said, "It was not to be Trevor. They were destined to die that day. You were not. Your dad knew you were the cornerstone a new world would be built upon. Violet is the key. It was imperative you both live. You went to the Island of Dreams to begin your training and Violet to the Place of Assassins to begin hers. If you had stayed you would be dead or in the hands of our enemies which would be worse."

He handed me a plate of food and I ate not knowing what I ate. Violet sitting beside me was shoveling food into her mouth automatically, knowing she needed sustenance and not caring what it was. We were both trying to accept the knowledge that our family had died saving us for a greater purpose. It did nothing to help heal the black hole in us. For the first time I understood why it needed to be healed. We needed to be whole and strong for what was to come. We looked into each others blue eyes and we both shivered with a sudden chill.

We finished our food and I looked around and found Georges and Analise sitting a little way away facing away from the fire watching the woods. They were close enough to hear what was said and far enough to not be distracted from their watch. There were empty plates at their feet so I knew they had eaten but not when. I was suddenly glad we had not come alone. We could not have handled this alone and we would have been sitting ducks. Dorian also knew things we would never have known on our own.

I set my plate aside, Violet did the same. We stood and she asked Dorian, "Tell us about the tree."

He banked the fire and nodded to Georges and Analise. We walked to the remains of the house where the tree grew tall through the middle of it with its spreading branches brushing the house logs. I noticed both Georges and Analise were armed and walked out away from us watching the forest. We approached the remains from the front where the porch used to be. It was completely gone and there was a gaping hole where the door used to be. We peered in and gasped at how beautiful it was. There was a thick mat of green grass dotted with unusual star shaped flowers, pure white with deep blue centers. The grass and flowers spread right into the corners of the logs that remained. Vines clung to the inside of the logs and had blue flowers in the shape of trumpets that shimmered in the breeze. I looked up the tree and was amazed at the size of it. Its girth was at least six feet around incredible for a twelve year old tree. It towered up and thick branches spread out to encompass the surrounding logs almost touching them. Thick green leaves and clusters of white flowers hung low. They made a room of soft green and white carpeted in green, white and blue. The flowers looked like scalloped bells all tied together and I thought I could actually hear them tinkling. It was not gloomy but shone with a gentle white greenish light that was comforting. I got the feeling it had been waiting for us and I could feel Violet felt the same.

In a daze I said, "Yes Dorian, tell us about the tree."

He continued; we had come too late to be of any help to your family. There were only two things we could still do, find and take Violet to the Palace and send your family on their way to the stars. The first task was not easy no one alive knew where Violet was. Our biggest fear was the enemy had taken her. We listened intently but heard nothing. We walked every inch of this ground and we feared the worst. Gabriel noticed an oddity in a small outside table that had been broken in the fight. Though broken two of its legs stood upright when they should have fallen over, they looked like they were leaning against something but were not. He started poking around the broken table and triggered a spring to a trap door that looked like the ground. It rose only an inch so it would not be seen if was sprung accidently. We pulled it open to reveal a tiny space and there curled up in a nest of blankets was Violet. We were all amazed at how small she was, she was curled around her hands on her chest, her eyes were closed and she had tears on her tiny face. Gabriel reached for her and her eyes popped open and they were such a fierce blue he pulled back. He reached for her again and pulled her from the pit she had survived in. He held her gently on his shoulder until she demanded to be put down.

We built the pyre for your family and laid them upon it all together after washing them and straightening their clothes. Violet picked flowers for each of the girls from their gardens, laying them upon their breasts and putting them in their hair. She picked a bouquet of all the flowers including her violets for your mother and laid it upon her breast never shedding a tear. She sprinkled fresh grass and pinecones mixed with flower petals around your father. She gazed at her family looked at us and nodded. She then asked for and was given a torch and Violet set the fire. When the fire cooled we took the ashes and first spread them in the remains of the house then on the gardens your mother had planted for each of her girls. It felt right to do so and you can see the growth in them is phenomenal as well as in the tree and there are no weeds anywhere.

The dead we dumped through out the forest leaving them to the animals. We could not leave them here where they would contaminate this ground.

The next full moon I was at the Palace of the Assassins having just brought Violet to begin her training. Gabriel came to me and said he had an assignment I needed to help him with. He showed me a packet that had a blue seed in it that glowed, he also had four buckets. He opened a door into this clearing and I followed him through. We dug a deep hole in the center of these logs and planted the seed. We covered it well and hauled water from the lake to water it. He said we could only use the lake water. Stream water would not do. For three days we walked the three miles back and forth hauling buckets of water from the lake. Our hands blistered and the sweat ran from our bodies. We had brought nothing to eat; Gabriel said the work was sustenance enough though we could drink, but only water from the lake. By the end of the third day we had made a small lake inside the burned walls. We knelt down to rest as the sun set behind the mountains, I remember my stomach aching from hunger. In the pearl gray dusk we heard a deep sucking sound and peering over the logs we saw the water being sucked into the hole where we planted the seed. When all the water was gone a small green sprout curled out of the hole and began to grow. In seconds it was inches, in minutes it was feet, in an hour it was yards tall and it kept growing until it towered over us. The leaves sprouted, the flowers bloomed. The grass and flowers grew and it has looked like this from then to now.

"What kind of tree is it?" I asked.

He answered, "It is a Tree of Truth.

Dorian, Violet and I stood and looked at the tree that was a tribute to everything Blue Eyes stands for; the Truth.

Then he said, "You must both sleep under the tree this night to know the truth. The truth will ease your heart and set you free."

CHAPTER TWENTY-EIGHT

Violet and I looked at each other and then turned and looked into the green tinted air beneath the tree, we felt it pulling and welcoming us into its depths.

We both knew we would sleep under the tree. We needed to check in with Castle Clarion first through Hope and be sure everything there was fine. Analise said she had peeked in on Hope and Jasmine throughout the day and heard nothing but happy babble. The time was near to check in with Jasmine. When we opened our doors she was waiting for us and Hope was excited to hear us. We babbled with Hope for a few minutes she was using more words every time we talked with her. Jasmine then filled us in on what was happening at the Castle which was nothing alarming only some funny antidotes which lightened our moods making us laugh.

It was getting dark when we finished with Jasmine and Hope. We had walked back to our campsite by the wood pile while we talked to them. Dorian was building up the fire to cook dinner. We told Dorian about Hope painting a tree on the nursery wall with strawberry pudding. She thought it was so pretty. He laughed then turned thoughtful.

"A tree huh?" He asked. "Did it have great spreading branches?"

I thought for a moment picturing the tree Hope had painted and realized it looked a lot like the Tree of Truth. I raised my eyebrows and looked at Dorian.

"We need to keep watch on that child," He said.

We all pulled food from our packs plus an extra pack cook had sent to make dinner. Dorian had a stew going within minutes as we all nibbled on hard rolls. Analise and Georges were still on guard but she had been thinking about Hope.

"Dorian, what kind of extra senses do you think Hope could have?" She asked.

He thought for a minute and said, "She could be an empath which means she would feel what those she is close to feels. If she is she will need to build shields to protect herself and soon. A wide open empath will feel everything good and bad. Because she is so young it will be limited but she needs shields or she will go mad with sensory overload."

We were all concerned with Hope she was such a sweet little girl and talked a bit about what we needed to watch for to keep her safe. Simply continuing with what we were doing would be telling enough. We talked about building shields, I had never built shields I had them from the Island of Dreams. The others didn't have the kind of shields Hope needed. Dorian said there was one at the Palace who could help her. I did not want her to go to the Palace of Assassins and he said she would come to her.

We were done eating and it was dark. We sat by the fire and I felt we were delaying the inevitable. We were going to sleep under the Tree of Truth because that was what we needed to do. So lets do it, and still I sat gazing into the fire. I slowly realized I was staring into the green glow of the Tree of Truth and Violet was standing next to me. Dorian, Analise and Georges were on guard behind us. We stepped into then walked under the tree looking up into its branches. I swore I could see eyes. My attention was taken by the trees branches as they grew and moved downward enclosing us inside its green glow. We could no longer see out and becoming sleepy lay down in the soft grass. I had the Black Sword with me and I laid it beside me. The ground conformed to our shapes for ultimate comfort. I could feel the grass, vines and flowers twining around us and the sword, bringing their fragrance with them as we slipped into a deep sleep.

Violet and I were dressed in white flowing pants and shirts and had Star flowers in our hair. The Black Sword was at my side it remained black but its scabbard was white. We walked through the soft mist of our lives as I was born and grew, father teaching and guiding me to independence at a young age. I was amazed at what I learned and never thought about. We watched as our sisters were born and joined the family learning all the things we needed to survive in our mountain world. Special attention was given to weaponry and survival skills. We also had picnics and chocolate cake, swimming lessons and games by the fire. We watched Violet born and I knew we were getting near the time we were both dreading to see. We could see that Violet was special from birth. She was alert to things around her walking and talking at a very young age. She had a small bow she was beginning to use and had excellent aim for a child just two, no wonder dad sent her to the Place of the Assassins.

I was walking down the path into that valley again and our lives were split each taking a different road. Dad intensified the girls training in self defense, even Violet was becoming lethal. I lay on the Island of Dreams and we saw what I was dreaming what dad had woven into that bag I was in. Defensive arts such as swordplay, staffs, bows, throwing stars and more I didn't even know I knew how to use yet. I had knowledge of peoples, leadership, and politics poured into my head. The use of doors and telepathy and other forms of magic I had yet to use were drummed into my very being until they were second nature. I knew when I needed them the knowledge would be there.

The day was sunny and peaceful, the Pigeon flew as we watched dad lower Violet into her hidey-hole he laid a hand on her head and her eyes closed. We knew this was not practice. This was the day. Dark men crept through the forest. Dad called to the girls where they were by the wood shed. They took up bows and quivers of arrows from the shed and strapped on swords and knives. They had on dark pants and colorful shirts with their long braids down their backs as they formed a defensive circle. Even five year old Daisy looked fierce and I felt immense pride in my sisters as they stood their ground and slowly moved as one toward the front of the house. Dad was cut off down by the stream. He was well armed but they went after him first. Mom looking like a Warrior Queen was on the front porch with Bow in hand and numerous arrows in buckets at her side and her sword strapped to her waist. They were so proud and valiant against overwhelming odds. They stood their ground and fought not for their own lives but for the little girl they had hidden away. The girl who was silently crying for her family she knew was lost. They fought silently every arrow finding its mark as the screaming attackers started piling up dead and the blood soaked the ground. Mother was a warrior with her blond braid down her back whipping back and forth as she took aim on those closest to her. Dad fought in a circle with his arrows gone, down to his sword in one hand and knife in the other bow forgotten on the ground. He had numerous wounds that were bleeding and still he fought on. He took a sword in the side and faltered as blood ran down his leg, he killed eight more before they got close enough to put a sword through his chest. They were about to fall on him to hack him to bits when a bolt of energy shot across the yard. They fell back leaving our father whole and bleeding out. His blood lovingly lapped up by this piece of earth we called home.

The girls had sustained wounds and were bleeding freely, we watched Daisy fall her blue eyes staring into a distance we could only guess at. Rose stepped protectively over her shielding her from more harm. Mom faltered on the porch when dad fell and an arrow found her side. She knew that her soul mate the other half of her soul was gone. She lurched to the side that the arrow had found, and then she straightened and knocked another arrow letting it fly. She was losing blood and growing weak as another arrow caught her in the thigh. Her knee buckled but she caught herself and let more arrows fly.

Rose was down lying protectively over Daisy and Lily was still shooting. She was wounded and using the rest of her sisters arrows when an arrow thumped into her chest and she fell onto her sisters. There were fifty or more men piled around them. The dark men had to climb over the fallen to look down on my sisters, the dead were piled upon the dead. Our mother the Warrior Queen knew her family was gone; she shot one more arrow then dropped her bow and bowed her head. The house was on fire behind her. An arrow took her high in the chest and she was dead before she hit the floor of the porch. This was the last dream I had on the Island of Dreams.

Our family was dead and we were stunned and numb. The hated Dark Man stepped out of the shadow. The men he had left which were few stood numb with exhaustion and not one was unwounded and bleeding. They looked at all their dead and then at the children, woman and man who had killed them all. I stared intently at them as they walked away. I appreciated they did not mutilate my family but if I ever again saw them somewhere I would know who they were.

The Yard was so quiet not even a bird made a noise. The logs of the house fell in and the fire went out and only a slim column of black smoke spiraled upward. Violet and I hugged each other grieving for our mother, father and sisters. We were also proud because they were brave, determined and fought so well because they loved us so much.

A door slid into being near the path to the lake and men poured silently out. I recognized Dorian and Gabriel and the dismay upon their faces turn to horror then deep sadness as they took in what was before them. They kicked aside bodies to get to the girls and my father. Someone picked our mother up and carried her off the burning porch. They laid her in the untouched grass and checked for life and slowly shook their head. The same slow shakes of a head accompanied each of the girls and my father as they were picked up and laid in the grass side by side. The search for Violet was on and Gabriel clicked the trigger to the door that held her in the ground.

CHAPTER TWENTY-NINE

We followed them through the scattering of the enemy. Preparations were made for the memorial and Violet lit the fire to send our family to the stars.

Violet climbed the 10,000 steps to the Palace of the Assassins and began her training. She was a fierce fighter and received no sympathy for either her circumstances or her age.

Dorian and Gabriel planted the Tree of Truth. I slept on the Island of Dreams. We watched events unfold as Violet was trained, to my escape, to our meeting and onward to the day we walked under the tree and lay sleeping. The black Sword began to sing in a soft sweet tune that was heart wrenching and a soft green mist enfolded Violet and me.

Out of the green mist came our family. Father, Mother, Lily, Rose, and Daisy came to us smiling and full of hugs and kisses for us. We were older then the girls and it didn't seem odd or different. It was good to see them though I didn't know how we were seeing them or touching them since they were dead. I could hear the Black Sword singing in the back ground and knew it had something to do with it and I was thankful. After hugs we sat on the ground and I knew we didn't have much time.

I looked at my family together again after all these years with tears in my eyes. I knew this would never happen again.

"I have some questions but before I ask them I want you to know something. I am proud to be the son and brother of the warriors you proved to be on that last day. I will always try to live up to the standards you have set." I said.

"As long as, you live," father said. And everyone laughed. I was a bit taken aback that they were laughing over their deaths. But, what else are you going to do?

"Dad," I began, "Why did you send me to the Island of dreams?" It was the one thing I needed to hear from him.

"Trev, son," he said, "I had one choice. You were walking into something you were not prepared to handle. I wanted you away from home when the Dark Man came calling for us. You had so much you needed to learn and I was out of time. I am adept at magic as you will become and the best place for you was the Island of Dreams. You needed to grow, become a man, and learn the things I would not be there to teach to do, the things you need to do. I wove a spell into that sleeping bag and sent that fog to carry you there. You are special son; and the world will not survive without you. It may not survive with you but you know the way to a new world if it comes to that. The Island of Dreams was the only choice."

I thought about that and said, "Thank you dad, I understand now. I was angry because I didn't grow up. I woke up a thirteen year old boy in a grown mans body with lots of knowledge that freaked me out."

"I didn't think about all the consequences, but you look like your doing OK, so I sand by my decision." He said.

"Yes I am doing great actually. I have Violet, good friends and I killed the Dark Man. Only there are more of them and he was the least." I said.

"That is the way it always is." He replied.

Violet said, "Father, why did you hide me?"

"You, Violet are as important to the salvation or destruction of this world as Trevor is. The two of you make a whole. Alone you are each just a person trying to stay alive. Together you are a force to recon with. You two are the lock and the key. The two of you will save this world or move on to another better one. To not save you, to let you die with us would have been unforgivable on our part. It would have meant no hope for this world but eternal damnation and us with it."

"Trevor," mom said, "Remember the painting, remember the door. Analise knows where it is. It may be your last and only choice. Both of you must live and we live through you for as long as you remember."

"Always stand back to back," dad said, "Watch out for each other, you both must live, remember, you both must live."

Lily said, "I would do it all over again to be sure you had a chance, if I wasn't already dead." And she laughed.

Rose said, "Don't worry about us and don't be sad. We are safe now. You're the ones who get to go through Hell."

Daisy stepped forward and said, "They are so weird and I have to spend eternity with them. Honestly Trevor and Violet we are so proud of the things you do. My favorite part was when you killed the Dark Man. He needed killing. We all love you and we were proud to know we kept you both safe. It made our lives worth the life we had. No regrets on our part."

Surprised I said, "Your favorite part was when I killed the Dark Man, you saw that?"

Lily said, "Of course silly what do you think we do among the stars?"

"We watch everything you do; it is so much fun to watch you." Rose said.

"We don't get to watch everything; we do have other things to do." Daisy admitted. "But we do love it when we do and we are all rooting for you."

Mom and dad stepped up and mom put her arms around the girls, and dad said, "That is quite enough, you are upsetting them a bit.

Dad reached out and pulled me to him in a hug and said, "I am proud of you son and I always will be no matter what. Give it your best shot it will be enough."

Dad held Violet at arms length and sighing said, "You look just like your mother the first time I saw her. I never thought there could ever be anyone as beautiful yet here you stand. You have powers deep within you, you have yet to tap. Dig deep Violet and you will be as effective as you are beautiful. I love you and I am proud of what you have done and will yet do." Dad stepped back with the girls.

Mom stepped forward and I knew time was short, I said, "Thank you." I gave her a hug only the love a son has for his mother can give and she returned it.

Violet looked at mom when I released her and said, "I miss you." And she fell to her knees in tears.

Mom knelt with her and said, "I know sweet heart. I will always be with you. I love you, I will always love you. When you look in the mirror, remember."

Violet looked up and said with tears running down her face, "I love you mom, I love you and I will remember."

Mom stepped back with dad and the girls and as they started to fade they called, we love you until they were no more.

As they faded Violet and I held each other and called, we love you, to them until they were no more.

I heard the song the Black Sword sang change. Violet and I opened our eyes at the same time looking at each other with the Black Sword between us. We smiled, at peace at last. The song changed again in urgency and we got to our feet as the tree rose from around us. The sun slanted down through the trees making it around noon. We saw Dorian, Analise and Georges with swords raised guarding the tree and facing a bunch of dark men. We saw the eyes of the men widen as we stepped forth from the tree. I with the Black Sword in hand, Violet with her Bow strung, arrow knocked. She took out the big man in front between Dorian and Analise and all three of our friends turned in surprise. We strode forward stepping between Georges, Analise and Dorian and men began to run. I lowered the Black Sword who had begun a battle song and energy poured from its tip. Violet raised her hand and energy poured from her palm. Those who were close disappeared. Those further away burned. Those even further away dropped dead. The rest ran and we let them.

Let them spread the word. Let them spread the terror. The evil men in this world needed to start being afraid.

We turned and faced our friends as one. We had become whole and we were lethal.

◆

CHAPTER THIRTY

Dorian stepped forward and said, "Are you two OK?"
We looked at each other and then back at him and nodded.

"Are you three OK?" I asked. "Good thing we came out just then. What were those men doing? You would have had trouble fighting that many."

"We already fought them once," Georges said, "They came back with more men."

Violet and I looked at each other surprised. We took a good look at our friends and realized they looked grubby. We then looked around and noticed everything looked slightly different like we had been here a while. How long have we been here?

So I asked, "How long have we been under the tree?"

"We were starting to get worried you would never come out," Analise said laying a hand on my arm and looking at me with worry, "Are you really OK?"

Dorian said, "Almost two weeks, that's how long you have been under the tree. If I had known before I would have had second thoughts. I have had second thoughts. We were making a plan to try to infiltrate the tree when this last bunch showed up. We got distracted trying to protect the tree and you. Then you show up and everyone starts disappearing, burning and running. What the hell happened?"

Violet and I looked at each other at a loss as how to explain. To my surprise Dorian stepped forward and gave me a great hug then he hugged Violet as violently.

"I told you we couldn't do this without you two then you disappear into a tree I planted and didn't come out. What was I to think, my god I am so glad you are back." He said. I had never seen Dorian so choked up over anything.

Georges said, "I for one am thrilled, can we go home?"

We all laughed and Violet and I looked around at our friends. We knew we had a lot of explaining to do but yes we needed to go home. We looked back at the Tree of Truth that still stood tall. We would never lie under its branches again but it still had purpose and we knew it had something to do with Hope. We both turned back to our friends noticing how fatigued they looked after standing guard over us for so long.

We walked to the camp we had set up grabbed our packs and I opened a door into the meadow below Castle Clarion.

"Let's go home," I said.

After almost two weeks of communicating with Jasmine and Hope, Analise had become adept at talking to them and letting them know what was happening on the spur of a moment. As we climbed the hill to the gate of the castle there were already people on the ramparts cheering at our return, though I wondered why. We were just returning from a camping trip. Cook was in the hall and informed us dinner would be served as soon as we cleaned up. The special dinner she had promised when we left. I had forgotten and hoped she had not gone to the trouble almost two weeks ago to have us not show up. I went to my room after greeting as many as I could and found a hot bath waiting. I lay the Black Sword on the bed and I dropped my clothes, I just now realized I smelled. The tub was full of hot water and I slipped into the bath with a contented sigh. I still used the hair soap for everything, I liked it. The towels were fluffy, my god they were fluffy. How, I still did not know. My beard was long and I had to do the scissors again so I could shave. After I was cleaned up I fell onto my bed and into a deep sleep griping the hilt of the Black Sword in my hand.

I dreamed of worlds, of our world. Our world scorched and desecrated by the Dark Men who I understood to not be men at all. I knew I must stop them, I must save our world. I also knew there were other worlds where we could flee and take refuge, worlds full of light and sun, mountains, valleys, waterfalls, clouds, rain, rainbows, prairies and all welcoming us. I knew there were worlds behind the golden door in the painting and in Analise's head. How many worlds would we destroy? They would come after us. If we fled there would come a day we could no longer run and we would have to fight and we would have to win or all would be lost. That would not be acceptable, loosing would never be acceptable. Running was just as unacceptable. Blue eyes swam into my vision, blue eyes stared me down. We were blue eyes and we will not loose.

I woke to the humming of the Black Sword and turned my head to look at it. It was clean and well oiled and urging me to get up. We had much work to do. But first a feast to attend!

I rolled out of bed and pulled the curtain aside, it was late afternoon so I had not slept over long. I pulled clothes from the closet choosing blue silk with black pants. I brushed out my hair and tied it back then picked up the Black Sword. Strapping it on I knew I would never go anywhere without it again, even a feast. I could feel Violet moving as if she was a second skin. She had also slept and we had woken at exactly the same time. We left our rooms and it felt like we were synchronized in all our movements. It creeped me out a bit so I decided to scratch my nose and she did not mimic me but I heard quietly, ["barbarian"] and I laughed. We were enmeshed as one but thankfully we could think and do things independently if my nose scratching meant anything. We needed to explore this more thoroughly to see just how connected we are and if it was going to get embarrassing. There are some things sisters should not be included in. ["Same here Bro."] I heard in my head.

We met at the entrance to the Great hall and simply nodded at each other before stepping in. I had noticed with disappointment that the painting of Analise and the door was no longer hanging at the end of the hallway. I had hoped to examine it more closely and wondered if I would ever see it again then knew I would. Somehow it was connected to everything happening and would help us in some way. The Dark Men came from somewhere and I didn't think they were from here. They had a way to travel from whatever world they were from and the Golden door was a key to how they did and how to stop them. I needed to find that painting.

We stepped into a room full of people. People we knew and had become our friends were there in the room and seemed genuinely glad to see us. We looked at each other and walked in step toward the future we could not yet see.

CHAPTER THIRTY-ONE

Cook out did herself and put on a feast no one was likely to forget ever. There were Honeyed Hams and a whole side of roasted beef. Roasted corn and new peas in cream sauce, pickled beets, rhubarb sauce, sliced pears and peaches sprinkled with raisins. There were potatoes and rutabagas, rolls of all kinds and cakes to make mouths water. There was even homemade ice cream. The ale and wine seemed to be especially excellent and I noticed some wine from the Snowy River country. I decided it was an excellent way to start a campaign to win a war.

Little Hope was there charming everyone and Jasmine was at attendance. We ate and we laughed and we looked at each other with grins and twinkles in our eyes. I knew the twinkles would soon go out but for now we were going to enjoy them.

Hope skipped up to me and said, "Grandma Tessa said I need to come and visit her real soon and you must bring me to the tree where she lives."

My hand stopped on the way to my mouth and my heart stopped in my chest. So this must be done before the end. Of course I should have known my family could help Hope to focus her thoughts and energy so as not to go insane with the feelings she has. The Tree of Truth still stood and Hope needed to go sleep and dream under its branches.

"Did she say how soon we must visit?" I asked

"She said you would know, and we could have fun!" Hope replied.

"OK, I will be sure to let you know in plenty of time." I said.

"Okey Dokey," She said and skipped off.

Violet came up and said, "What was that all about?"

"Hope says we are or she actually is going to see grandma Tessa and we have to take her. She will have fun and we will know when." I replied.

"Soon, she is struggling with the feelings she picks up everywhere and she will be lost if mother doesn't help her. So soon we travel back to the Tree of Truth this time to guard, and guard someone so precious and I believe valuable in what lies ahead of us all. I wish I was a precog like father so I knew what was going to happen." She said.

"Have you tried?" I asked. "We both have so many talents that are latent and just waiting to pop out, how do you know you aren't?"

Violet thought for a minute and then said, "I'll keep my mind open." She got up and walked over to Georges sitting down and taking up the conversation.

Analise sat down and said, "Why suddenly so gloomy?"

"We are taking Hope to the Tree of Truth." I said. "She is to meet Grandma Tessa."

"OH!" Analise said. "So when is this happening?"

"We will know." I said.

"Why is that always the answer?" She asked.

"I guess because things happen when they do for good reason and shouldn't happen before." I answered. "We need to find the painting of the Golden Door, it may be our last hope and I have been assured you know where it is."

"Whoever told you that is misinformed." Analise said.

"My mother is pretty accurate and considering where she gets her information these days I assure you, you do know where it is.

We just need to figure out how to access that information in your Psyche." I replied.

Analise sat back hand over her mouth, green gold eyes wide in shock. She said, "Oh my, that's where you got your information? If your mother told you I know where it is then I must. How can I know and not know?"

"Probably the same way Violet and I keep doing things we didn't know how and suddenly could, someone put it in your subconscious." I said.

"Someone messed with my brain?" She asked not looking at all happy.

"I wouldn't say messed with your brain, just inserted something you will need in the future when they will no longer be there. It had to be someone who loved you very much to give you something in a place where it would never be lost, information that could mean our and your salvation and continued life." I said.

"I like thinking about it like that, but how do I access this information I have that I don't remember?" She asked.

"Good question, maybe you should visit my mother with Hope. I believe she could help you know where to go and I would like you to meet my mother. You will also be there for Hope. Good idea, OK, that's settled, lets go talk to Dorian, Georges and Violet. I believe it is time for the visit to my mother, I wonder if Hope knew?" I said.

I pulled a stunned Analise to her feet and over to where Georges and Violet sat. Dorian walked in just then so I knew we were on the right track. I motioned him to our table and we all sat down.

Violet said, "So you found the missing piece? The morning will be soon enough for us to go. I'll bet that little rascal is already packed and has her favorite teddy bear on stand-by."

"Precog? Yes, Analise needs to see mother as well as Hope. Hope needs to have someone with her and only someone in need can go. Mother can help Analise remember where the painting of the Golden Door is. We need that painting; it could be our salvation and mean the lives of many. We also need Hope alive and well, mother can do that." I said.

Dorian sat stunned with this new information and I am sure the news that we would be going back to the Tree of Truth so soon. He simply nodded and got up to get a plate of food. Georges was also stunned.

"What if the Dark Men come back and we have to fight them again. Can we fight that many?" Georges ever practical asked.

I looked at him and said, "Analise and Hope will be under the tree. I and Violet will be with you and Dorian on guard outside the tree. Believe me Georges when I say nothing will get through to the tree or anywhere near it. The Dark Men will know who stands guard and will not want a repeat of the last time they tried an attack on the Tree of Truth." I said.

I suddenly realized just how precious the lives were who would be sleeping under the tree. Hope, yes we would need that little girl though I knew not how. Analise I realized I could not live without. I was shaken to my core and visibly trembled thinking about Analise being vulnerable and the possibility of losing her. No, never, it will never happen, she will always be here and she will always be mine and that thought shook me even more. That she would be mine. I heard Violet call, ["What?"] and I slammed that door shut. What was I feeling? What was I doing? Analise, I could not lose Analise and with that truth I knew I was lost. Turning I looked deep into those green and gold eyes and I knew we were both lost. We held each others gaze then we both nodded and turned back to the table. Violet was looking at me with raised eyebrows as if saying, about time. I shrugged and flicked a grin at her and got up to get some more ice cream and chocolate cake, you can never have too much ice cream and chocolate cake.

CHAPTER THIRTY-TWO

People started drifting out heading back to their rooms. The five of us were finishing a last glass of wine after praising cook for her wonderful feast. We told her we would be going back to the Tree of Truth tomorrow and whatever she could wrap up for us would be appreciated. She just shook her head and started giving order on what to wrap up for us. We bid the last of our friend's good night and stood up to head for our own beds. We had agreed to meet in the Great Hall at 6:00 the next morning which didn't give us a lot of sleep. We split up Analise and I heading down the same hall. We walked past my door and I walked her to hers. She turned to say goodnight and I leaned in and kissed her. I didn't think, I just felt and I felt I could kiss this girl, woman, Analise forever. I leaned into her and she leaned into me. There was a click as the door knob turned and we were in her room with the door shut and sprawled across the bed. I was drowning in kisses as my head swam and the world spun. Nothing had ever tasted so wonderful or felt so good and it hit me like a brick to the head; I love this woman, I love Analise. With that thought I kissed her even deeper and didn't care if I ever came up. We were wrapped in each others arms when we finally tilted our heads back to look into each others eyes.

"I love you," We both whispered at the same time. She snuggled her head down on my shoulder, I pulled a blanket over us and we fell into a deep sleep.

There was a great pounding on the door, and then the door hit the wall. We both sat up stunned the blanket falling away to reveal we were both still dressed which was good since it was Dorian standing there.

Dorian yelled, "I can't find Trevor!" He paused, "I found Trevor." He took in the situation then said, "I wish you would inform if not me at least someone when you are not going to sleep in your own room."

"I'm sorry," I said, really concerned because he was right. "It just sort of happened."

Analise nodded not knowing what to say. Then she looked at me and said, "From now on we will plan better and let people know if we will be in your room or mine."

Dorian looking dumbfounded at that, said, "Breakfast is ready." He then turned and left purposely closing the door.

I looked at her and smiled then leaned over and kissed the corner of her mouth then the top of her breast that was peaking out of her dress.

"Breakfast awaits my love." I said smiling at her. She stretched her arms above her head doing wonderful things to her body and mine by default.

"Are you sure you want breakfast?" She asked.

Hell no I didn't want breakfast all I wanted was her as I consumed her with my eyes. I rolled off the bed standing up and picking up my boots I don't remember taking off. I picked up the black sword I did remember laying on the long bench at the foot of the bed.

"I do want you to meet my mother." I said. "Time flies and we don't have much left. The Tree of Truth waits. I am surprised the Dark Men have left us alone this long. Dress to travel and I'll see you in the Great Room."

I left her room and headed back to my own to change and grab my pack, coat and hat. I also packed my gun after checking it. This was an important trip with very important people; I would use the gun if I had to. Satisfied I nodded my head and headed to the great room. I felt different, older as if I had grown into my age and it felt good. The first person I saw was Violet; she smiled and nodded then turned back to Georges. For the first time I questioned their relationship. Now that I was beginning one with Analise I wondered what was going on with my little sister and Georges. ["Don't even go there Bro. I am far older then you by years of experience and what I do with whomever is my business."]

OK, I won't go there besides I like Georges. I started scanning the breakfast food picking up a cinnamon roll and some fruit when I felt her walk into the room. I turned and wondered how anyone could look so beautiful in a pair of green hiking pants with a silk shirt that matched and of all things green boots. Her hair was pulled back and braided down her back making her eyes stand out and sparkle like emeralds. ["You're drooling."]

["Shit, we need to make some rules or something so you don't keep invading my head."] I said.

["It's called a door, very useful you close it and people on the other side can't hear you broadcasting lust. Congratulations on growing up by the way. Your thoughts are healthier."] She said.

["Healthier?"] I shut the door.

Hope burst into the room squealing with delight that she was going to see her grandma. She lives in a tree she told everyone then she spotted me. Rushing up to me she paused and gave me a grave look.

"You are different." She stated just as Analise walked up to us. She looked at Analise and then back to me. "You two are in love. Don't let it overwhelm or distract you or all is lost. Love has lost more then worlds and lives but these are our lives that would be lost and we wish to keep them."

Startled I looked at Analise whose face was white with shock. She knelt down and said to Hope, "We will be on guard and you and our friends will watch and tell us if we are too involved to see what is important."

Hope nodded sagely then asked, "Are there muffins?"

Analise took her by the hand and they went together to find breakfast. I turned and Jasmine was standing there looking at me.

"Is it that obvious?" I asked.

"Only to those who know you well and to Hope she sees everything, it is good she is going to your mother at this time. Her abilities are growing by leaps and she is hard to keep up with. I fear for her." She said.

"Her speech has improved greatly, she doesn't even sound like a two year old. When did this start to happen?" I asked.

"It didn't start happening it just happened. She woke up one morning with the speech patterns and vocabulary of someone much older. It was as if she learned it in her sleep, is that even possible?" She asked.

I thought of the Island of Dreams and decided her rooms needed investigating when we returned. Something was going on unless it is all internal but still something was going on. I walked back to the food with Jasmine and grabbed some eggs and ham to go with what I had. I set my food at a table where Dorian and Georges sat and went back to get coffee. Analise and Hope was at table when I got back and Jasmine came up juggling a full plate and hot coffee. I grabbed her coffee so it didn't spill it and she sat with us.

I glanced at Analise and Hope then turned to Jasmine who would not accompany us and asked, "Are you doing something special with your holiday?"

"I plan on visiting my husband's family. I have not spent much time with them since his death and it feels good to do it at this time." She replied.

"Where do they live, anywhere near here?" I asked.

"About half a days ride south in a bit of a village called Heavenly Cart. Probably because the first person who rode in a cart there thought it was heavenly." And she laughed. "Seriously they are very down to earth people; it will be good to see them again. They are one of the last villages to pack up and come to the castle and I plan on helping them pack. They have believed for too long they are safe this close to the castle.

Scraping up the last of my food I said, "I hope you have a wonderful time and are able to get them on the move. It is not safe outside the castle." Jasmine grinned and nodded turning thoughtful.

"Soon as breakfast is over," I said looking at everyone else, "we need to gather our packs and head to the meadow I would like to get started soon."

We all rose and went to find our packs where ever we had stashed them. Jasmine touched my arm, "You will take care of her won't you? I have become very fond of our little Hope." She asked.

"With my life, I swear. We will all be back soon and the little dear will be back in your charge and babbling your ear off. And you will encourage your in-laws to pack quickly and get back to the castle." I said.

Jasmine nodded and turning walked away. I watched as she went and she seemed to disappear into a mist. I shook my head and thought that was weird. I went to find my pack and found everyone at the front of the Great Hall waiting for me. We walked out into the slush; the snow was melting since spring was on the way. Hope was talking about seeing her grandma holding Analise's hand so she didn't stumble. I made the decision to open a door right into the yard of the cabin where the Tree of Truth resided. Hope was too small to walk from the lake besides it held no memories for her. Jasmine had put her blond hair up in little pony tails on top of her head. She had on her best dress and was carrying her favorite doll. She looked adorable and I knew my mother was going to love her.

Chapter Thirty-Three

I opened the door outside the gate and Hope gasped as she looked through the gate. It was a beautiful sight, the tree reaching for the sky that was an incredible blue the trees branches spreading up and out bowing under the weight of hundreds of flowers. The logs surrounding the tree had flowers climbing all over them and the flower beds beside them were a riot of brilliant color in full bloom. The yard in front of the dilapidated cabin was covered in a deep green grass filled with wild flowers. We stood there looking into this most beautiful place filled with peace. I stared in wonder that I grew up here in this cabin in such beauty. We stepped through the door and were overwhelmed with the clean light fragrance of mountain air and flowers. We could hear birds chirping and the wind sighing through the tall pine trees that surrounded the area. Seeing movement I turned my head to see several deer delicately picking their way through a clearing in the woods their heads turning ears twitching alert for danger. They hadn't sensed us yet then Hope who had been silent with awe burst out with laughter so pure it surprised me and made me laugh. The deer zeroed in on us then bounded off through the sun dappled woods to another quieter place.

Violet said, "I sense no danger, all is as it seems."

We headed over to where we made camp last time near the old wood shed. The fire ring was there and a small pile of wood we had left was piled near by. We sat down our packs and I asked Hope if she wanted to do some exploring with me. She jumped up and down in excitement making us all smile; there is something infectious about a small child's joy and laughter.

Even though we all felt peaceful and felt no danger we stayed on high alert, we all knew things could change very quickly. I took Hopes hand and we started with the stream looking at the water spiders and watching the minnows swimming in the little pool. Hope tried to catch them and squealed with laughter as they slipped away swimming around her little hands just out of reach as if it was a fish dance just for her. Her laughter reminded me of another little girl doing the exact same thing. I looked up at Violet and knew she was remembering the same thing. We had kept our doors shut tight and so I said, ["It's OK to remember Violet, to see through the eyes of a child what you did as a child and to know you were happy."]

["I miss them so much and I had so little time with them and I remember Hope had even less time with her family. It makes me hate the Dark Men so much I want to kill them all for what they did, for what they are doing."]

["We will stop them Violet, hopefully in this world. I want this world to survive but if it is not to be we will stop them in the next. They will come after us since we dare to stand up to them when they think they will crush us but we will be ready and I promise they will die."]

Hope laughed again and said, "Good I want them to die too, all of them."

Violet and I looked at each other in amazement; we thought we were being discreet and the little tyke heard everything we said. ["Hope can you answer me telepathically."]

Laughing again as a fish slipped through her fingers she said, ["Of course Unca Trev, I always hear you but this is the first time you asked me to answer."]

["Can you shut me out so you can't hear me?"] I asked.

["I have to, you talk too much."] She said laughing.

Violet and I looked at each other and Violet said, "She has a natural shield by necessity evidently you talk too much."

"You talk too much to, Auntie Violet." Hope said.

We all laughed and I suggested we go look at the flower gardens. I told her about each of our sister and how they were named after flowers. Lily Jane, Rose Ellen, Daisy Jean and Violet Marie, when they were born our mother planted a flower bed in their honor with their flower. I told her how brave each one was and how we missed those who were gone but we knew they were watching over us and cheering for us. The flowers were beautiful and Hope could not decide which one was her favorite. I told her she didn't have to have a favorite she could love them all. She solemnly nodded her head and agreed she did love them all.

Dorian called saying it was time for lunch and we made our way back to the wood shed yard and the fire pit there. Dorian had laid out cold meats, breads, fruits and raw veggies Cook had packed. He had a fire going and we had hot coffee and Hope had hot chocolate. She was yawning hugely after lunch so Analise suggested she lay down for a few minutes to rest her eyes. She snuggled into her sleeping bag beside the fire with blinking eyes and was sound asleep in minutes. We sat around talking about inconsequential things while she slept which was longer then usual since she had such an early busy morning. When Hope woke up we explored the woods finding deer and a fox family. There were lots of birds to watch and the trees themselves were beautiful. Both Violet and I noticed the absence of dead Dark Men. Either the animals were efficient or they disappeared another way and neither one of us liked that thought. We spent a lazy after noon laughing and playing. We played catch with pinecones which Hope was quite adept at for her age. We tried to skip stones on the stream but we really needed the lake for that but did not want to hike that far away from the Tree.

The sun was going down when we walked into the clearing behind the cabin from the woods. We all pitched in to make dinner that was delicious. And then we were soon standing in front of the Tree of Truth. It was dark out by now but somehow it was lit under the tree. I looked up and could see thousand of stars twinkling in the night sky and I wondered which ones were other planets we could live on. I focused on the tree again and saw that Analise and Hope were already standing under the Tree and wondered how that happened. I tried to step forward and could not. I stared to panic but Violet intervened by saying, ["There is nothing you can do for them now, they are on their own. Mother will take care of them."] I stood and watched the tree close down around them and had an inkling of how my three friends who watched the tree close over Violet and I had felt. Utterly helpless, all we could do now was stand guard over the Tree of Truth and the ones we loved sleeping beneath it. I reached out trying to feel Analise and Hope so I would know they were alright but there was a great emptiness as though they had never existed. That was almost my undoing and I fell to my knees Black Sword clutched in my hand and it was singing softly almost a lullaby as if to soothe me.

CHAPTER THIRTY-FOUR

Violet knelt in front of me saying, "It's OK Trevor, Analise told me she tried to reach out to us when we were under the tree and could feel nothing. We would know if they were not alright, the Tree would let us know."

I slowly rose to my feet looking around. Dorian and Georges were on lookout facing toward the woods about 30 feet away. The woods were dark and anything could be out there. The clearing had dropped into darkness when the Tree closed and was lit only with starlight, enough to see each other by. It was going to be a long night; actually I didn't know how long it would be. Violet and I was under the Tree for almost two weeks. I hope fervently it would not be that long. How Dorian, Georges and Analise were able to stand not knowing that long, I didn't know.

Violet said in my head, ["We stand what we have to and we wait as long as necessary."]

I thought about that and knew she was right; there was nothing else we could do but wait. I knew I would wait till the end of time for Analise. We walked over to Dorian and Georges joined us. We were all alert and looking out for danger scanning the dark woods constantly.

Quietly I said, "We need to set watches, four hour increments. Who ever is off watch during meal times, cooks. Dorian, you and I will take the first watch from now till one hour after midnight. Georges and Violet get some sleep we will wake you then."

Georges and Violet headed for camp and Dorian looked at me before taking his station.

"She will be fine, Trev. They will be back before you know it. Analise with information on the Golden Door and little Hope with her Psyche firmly in place. It seemed like you and Violet were gone forever when you were under the Tree. Waiting is the hard part then suddenly you were there and the waiting was over. You're just so damned glad they are back it seems like no time at all passed." He said.

"Thanks Dorian, I am realizing they, especially Analise mean more to me then I knew. I don't know what I would do without her." I said.

"Hide it; if you truly love her as I think you do you must hide your feelings. If the Dark Men knew your feelings for Analise they would stop at nothing to take or hurt her to get to you. Hide your feelings and keep her safe. There will be plenty of time after this is over to show her you love her." He said.

What he said hit me like a ton of bricks falling from the sky. I staggered and would have fallen if he had not grabbed my arm. How could I be so stupid, of course they would go after her if they knew I loved her. She had to be protected at all costs, life would have little meaning with out her and I could not imagine a world without those green eyes.

"Yes, Dorian you are right. Gods man what am I to do?" I asked.

"Distance yourself; concentrate on the war and getting as many people as possible to safety in a new world if necessary. We have a lot of planning to do and Kingdoms to contact. If we have to make an exodus it can't be spur of the moment, people need to know what to do." He said.

I nodded my head and walked to my post as he took up his. I could think while I watched and I really needed to think about all this. I needed to talk to Analise I could not just start ignoring her, her reaction to me doing that would be as much a tell tale as mooning over each other. She needed to be on board with this, we had to go back to being companions in war. I knew we could do that to protect each other, we would do anything. I wondered what they were doing right now then forced my self to begin planning an escape for as much of the Kingdoms as we could.

Analise and Hope was lying beside each other hand in hand under the Tree of Truth. Hope was clutching her favorite doll and they were having tea with Trevor's mother Tessa under a tree in the front yard of the cabin with the red front door. The cabin was whole again and they could hear noises inside from Trevor's three sister and father in the kitchen.

Hope had shown grandma Tessa her doll and she was impressed with how pretty she was and how well Hope took care of her. Tessa offered Hope a small cake with pink icing, Hopes favorite color. Hope glanced at Analise who nodded then crammed it into her mouth. Tessa and Analise both laughed and Hope grinned around pink icing. Hope swallowed then took a drink of her milk and gave them a real smile.

Tessa said, "Analise it is so nice to meet and spend time with the woman my son is in love with."

Analise looked startled then a beautiful smile spread over her face. Of course his mother would know and she hoped she would meet whatever standards his mother had set for her sons mate. She loved Trevor and would not give him up for anyone.

"I can see you love him every bit as much as he loves you." Tessa continued. "You have nothing to worry about; we have known you and he would fall in love long before you talked to him as a boy. You two were destined to be together."

Analise's eyes opened in surprise and she said, "You knew? How could you know we were meant for each other?"

"Everything is written in the stars, we see what we are meant to see." She replied. "Just as I see you must hide how you feel and what you mean to each other."

Analise was even more surprised, "But why? Why do we need to hide our love? We just found it and now you say we have to tuck it back away from us?"

"Yes and when you truly think about it you will agree. Think Analise about what the Dark Men will do when they find our how you feel about one another. They will do whatever it takes to kidnap, hurt or even kill you to cripple Trevor. If he cannot do what he must over worry of you this world will fall and everyone in it will die. There will be no new world to escape to because he will not be able to save anyone if you are gone. He will become rage and rage kills everything even the good." Tessa said.

Hope looked up with pink icing on her cheek and said, "Grandma is right Ana, you must hide how you feel or we will all die and you will be first. You must hide it deep."

Analise and Tessa both looked at the cute little girl and Tessa got the first inkling of what she needed to do to keep this little girl intact. Analise knew that they were right and she would need help to pull it off. The price of their love was too high at this time, so it would have to wait.

"Let's take a walk." Tessa said. "The lake is beautiful this time of day. Do you know how to skip stones Hope?"

"Nope, I don't even know what that is." Hope said.

"We will teach you, I know Analise can skip stones." She said.

CHAPTER THIRTY-FIVE

The walk to the lake didn't seem to be three miles as Analise knew it was. Tessa must have shortened it knowing Hope would be tired out by such a long walk. Time and space was different under the Tree and easily manipulated by those who knew how. The two women showed Hope how to pick the stone just right to get the best and most skips. Tessa and Analise impressed Hope by finding the perfect stone needed, round and flat and thrown just a certain way, which they both demonstrated. She jumped up and down and laughed clapping her hands, she then stared to search for her own perfect stones. The little girl made a pile and started to practice. Soon her tongue was hanging out the side of her mouth in concentration. She said it was harder then it looked but soon was throwing stones with four and five skips.

Tessa sat on a large rock not to far away from Hope and started to take advantage of Hopes concentration. Using the talent within herself that allowed her to strengthen the superior traits in others she projected energy into the little girl. With every skip of a stone she imbued the little girl with an affirmation of her innate goodness, intelligence and gifts that made her special. She worked hard with every skip to tack the child's Psyche firmly in place giving her the strength to accept who she was and what she could do without being overwhelmed or going insane by what she could accomplish at such a young age. Tessa could see Hope was already starting to unravel by her abilities and her inability to accept them as young as she was. She was an old soul in a small child. She put time constrains on abilities too advanced for her, to become active at a time later in the child's life when she was mature enough to handle them. Tessa was amazed at the abilities the child held within her small frame and knew someday she would be a force to recon with. The Dark Men must never find out about this child. It would be better if she were dead then they get their hands on her. With every skip of a stone she used her energy as she worked and strengthened this small child she now loved and admired for who she would become.

Hope knew something was happening to her every time she skipped a stone and she knew it was helping her. She thought Grandma Tessa had something to do with it or was it skipping stones? She felt better then she had in a long time. Stronger, healthier and happier, she laughed with pure joy because of how she felt and how well she could skip stones. Hope was gaining the ability to be a child again and the joy that comes from being a child. Her adultness and the worries and cares that come with the knowledge she was carrying was slipping away with each skip. She retained enough to be who she was and she knew everything was still there just put in boxes to be opened later. The presence in her head slowly receded and she stopped skipping stones and turned to Tessa.

Hope walked up to Tessa took her hand and kissed it. She said, "Thank you Grandma, you are the greatest gift I have ever had. I'm hungry."

Analise turned from the lake where she had also been skipping stones and she and Tessa both laughed. They then heard singing and laughing coming down the path from the cabin. A booming mans voice and several girls voices all mixed together.

They stepped onto the sand by the lake from the woods and the man called, "Who's hungry? We come bearing food and drink from the great cabin in the wood. A picnic it is to be and the best part is the chocolate cake."

They swooped toward the two women and child with their baskets and smiles.

The man bowed before Hope and said, "I am your grandpa Teague sweet little girl." Turning to Analise he said, "I hope you will think of me as father as I am to Trevor, but you may call me Teague." He then kissed her cheek and smiled.

Each of the girls stepped up with a smile and introduced themselves hugging both Analise and Hope. Daisy the youngest asked Hope if she wanted to help her spread out the blanket.

"You always need a blanket to sit on when you have a picnic." Daisy explained, "Or you get sand in your food and that's gross."

Lily and Rose set the food out in the middle of the blanket and they all sat down around it. Tessa passed out plates filled with fried chicken, potato salad, and fresh rolls. She pointed out fresh fruit cut up in a bowl you could help yourself to when you wanted. Everyone dug into the food saying how good it was. The bowls and plates were getting empty as they started to slow down and take their time sitting back observing one another.

Hope spoke up and said, "I saw your flower gardens. I couldn't decide which flower I liked best. Unca Trev says I can love them all the same because he does. I can see why he loves you so much, you are an awesome family. I wish I could remember my mom like he does you."

Analise's heart wrenched for her, being found in a pile of dead bodies was not a good way for a child to remember her family and she had no memories from before then.

"Well I just happen to have a special guest to go with our chocolate cake." Teague said. He looked over our shoulders down the beach. We all turned and could just make out a woman strolling along the water with the setting sun at her back. We could make out a long fall of wavy golden hair and a long dress over a slim form. She became clearer as she came closer and we could make out the laser blue eyes that looked just like Hopes in a beautiful face that someday would be Hopes face. She had a big smile and tears in her eyes as she approached our picnic. Hope stood in shock, and then she screamed Mama, and ran for the woman almost knocking her over in her joy at seeing the woman she was just wishing she could remember.

Hope was picked up and swung around and around and covered in kisses. The woman then came up carrying Hope holding her tight.

"Thank you," she said, "I never thought I would see her again. I didn't even know if she would survive the drug or the massacre. Thank you so much for giving me this time with her."

Tessa rose and went to the woman saying, "Please come and sit we have chocolate cake and memories to share.

She came and sat introducing herself as Rianna. She told us how she knew the Dark Man was coming to their village and she knew no way to escape but her daughter must live if at all possible. She told us about the blue flower that grew in the woods she ground adding it to her bottle to put the baby to sleep. If given enough it could slow your system enough to mimic death, too much and it was death. She gave the baby the lesser amount and took the full amount herself. She knew if she was taken they would find her blue eyes and that would be a disaster. They had not been there long; they were trying to keep ahead of the Dark Man. They had a small house on the edge of the village and her husband had gone on ahead to find the next place they could go. He had been gone too long, then it was too late. She assumes he was taken or dead, since he is not here he must be a prisoner. All she could do was hope his eyes were hidden from the Dark Man. She reached over and squeezed Analise's hand then thanked her for taking care of her baby.

Analise said, "Watching over Hope has been a pleasure. How did you hide your blue eyes?"

"My husband and I wore brown contacts and I wouldn't let anyone near enough to my daughter to see her eyes." She said.

Teague asked, "What was your surname? I know all the Blue Eyes and I don't recall you or your husband."

Rianna blushed then raised her head and said, "It no longer matters we are all gone now. I prefer my daughter to keep the name she has. It is a good omen and will protect her." She gave her daughter a fierce hug telling her it was OK.

Tessa served chocolate cake all around with milk poured from a jug. It was delicious and we all ate two pieces. Teague said he was going to make ice cream but couldn't figure out how to keep it cold. Hope said that was OK, she had ice cream last night. Everyone laughed and said how lucky she was. She gave us all a big chocolate grin and nodded her head. Her mother took her to the lake to wash her face. They knelt at the edge of the lake face to face for a few minutes; Hope gave her a big hug and got one in return. When they came back Rianna said it was time for her to go. We all rose and gave hugs all around.

When she hugged Analise she held her tight and said, "Take care of my baby, Hope is a good name for her because she is all my hope. I will be watching when I can and cheering for all of you."

She bent one last time and with tears in her eyes she picked Hope up holding her for a last few minutes she whispered, "I love you Hope. You are my Hope, you will do great things in your life and you make me proud. Remember I will always love you and watch over you. Look into the stars and I will be looking back. I love you."

Hope said through her tears, "I love you too mommy. I will remember and I will make you proud."

Rianna handed Hope to Analise and walked away into the last sliver of the setting sun from where she had come never looking back. The rays of the setting sun turning her into a silhouette and then engulfing her completely as though she had never been.

Hope looked at Analise and drying her tears said, "Momma says you're my momma now and I have lots of good people to look after me. She said I need to be a good girl and she will be watching me. I'm glad I have you Ana, I love you. I'm tired." She opened her mouth in a huge yawn, put her head on Analise's shoulder and fell asleep.

Chapter Thirty-Six

The picnic was packed and they were back at the cabin in quick time. Lily took Analise into the cabin and showed her where to lay Hope down for a nap. Analise didn't realize how heavy the little girl had gotten until she put her down. She stood and leaned back to stretch her back muscles.

Lily said, "I will watch over her. Mom and dad are waiting for you under the tree in the yard."

Analise gave her a quick hug saying, "I am glad I got to know you a little. You are a beautiful person Lily, you all are." Lily smiled as Analise left the little room to her and Hope. She smelled fresh coffee before she got to the table under the tree and gave a soft sigh. Coffee sounded just right.

Analise sat down and Teague handed her a cup of coffee and asked, "How is my son?"

Analise thought a minute tipping her head back and noticing the tree had tiny white lights all through it making a soft light around them all at the table. She answered, "Stressed trying to carry the world on his shoulders. Trying to make the best decisions for us all, delegating when he can but he takes the brunt of it all himself. He is growing into himself; you can no longer see the thirteen year old boy in the man he has become. He has become one with the Black Sword and they work together with grace and lethal beauty. You would be proud of him, he is strong."

"I am proud of him; he was trained to be strong besides he carries it in his genes. What about love, has he learned to love?" He asked.

"Yes he has. His heart is so big sometimes I worry he loves too much. He loves me." Analise said.

"That worries you doesn't it?" Teague asked.

"Everything could be lost because of his love of me," She said,

"Do you believe you have such power?" He asked.

"It is not my power, if the Dark Man should learn of this love and kill or kidnap me Trevor would tear the world apart in his rage. He is capable of great rage. He keeps it in reign but if something should happen to me he will not hold it in. He will let it fly and whoever stands in its path will be destroyed. I would not want to see such a thing happen." She replied.

"My son does love greatly. I do believe he holds such rage; with the Black Sword as his partner he will do well if it is directed toward the evil filling our world. But you fear otherwise?" He asked.

"Yes, I do." She answered.

"Would you consider hypnosis as a means to dismiss the love you have for my son until such a time it is safe for you to express it?" Teague asked.

"I would do anything to keep Trevor and our people safe." Analise answered.

"You say people and not world." He said.

"I do not hold much hope for this world. The Dark Men are entrenched and my only hope is we can save some of it." Looking at the two of them she then said, "Which brings me to the Golden Door. I believe you can tell me where it is or help me find the Door to other worlds. It may be the only way we can save anything of our world by traveling to another. I have seen the painting and I know I am connected to it I just don't know how to find it."

"Actually you do know where it is." Tessa said. "Its location is in your head. It is hidden much the same way your love for Trevor will be hidden. All you need is the trigger word spoken in a certain way and you will remember."

Analise was surprised and unable to speak for a few minutes. She then asked, "Who did this to me, and why?"

Teague answered, "I did. Though I did not foresee the paintings need to be seen and its ability to pop on and off walls creating a ghost painting myth. It has been interesting."

"Interesting?" Analise asked. "You think it's been interesting? I have been hearing of and occasionally seeing the painting my whole life and wondering why it does what it does and you think it's interesting?"

"Yes I do find it interesting as well as your reaction." He laughed a hearty laugh then said, "We can never know the affect our plans can have."

"So what we do to affect the love I have for Trevor could also have side affects?" She asked.

"Absolutely though I imagine any affect will be small since I believe you are truly in love and nothing can subvert that for any length of time. Love will out, as they say." Teague said.

"Love will out. I won't hate him or anything will I? I couldn't stand it if I hated him, though I guess I wouldn't know any different. I still don't want to hate him; all I really want to do is love him." She said in despair.

Taking pity on her Tessa said, "No dear, you will not hate him only think of him as a brother with possibly flashes of love you'll think are weird."

"OK, I could do that. When can we start and when can I hear this word you put in my subconscious?" Analise asked.

"Lean back and close your eyes." Teague said. "Think of the tallest peak the sun comes over first thing in the morning and how it makes you feel. How it fills you with joy at the start of a new day and how happy you are at that moment. You are relaxed and happy to sit in your chair and revel in the rising of the sun thinking about Trevor and what a nice guy he is. He is a great older brother figure you never had though irritating at times. You run through his virtues and his faults and realize no matter what, he is just irritating. A big older brother who is irritating, you will believe this until you hear Diablo whispered in your ear on a dark and starless night. Next I am going to whisper a word in your ear under this tree with the white lights on and you will wake and remember where the painting of the Golden Door is."

"Ribbitt." He whispered.

Analise woke and said, "Ribbitt. I remember that word. When I was a little girl I used to think that was what frogs were saying. I remember telling you that under this very tree, I even spelled it for you. I remember you two and this house. How old was I when I came here?"

Tessa answered, "You were just four years old and the painting needed to be hidden from prying eyes. You gave us the cue to unlock your mind as to where it is hidden. You now know where it is so you and Trevor can use it to travel to another world with everyone you can save if necessary."

"He is so irritating; do you really think he will listen to me? Even if we find the painting do you think he will use it? Trevor is such a know it all. I know he is your son but really he can be irritating." She said.

Tessa and Teague looked at each other and smiled. Tessa thought, ["Let's hope it is going as well with Dorian as it did with us."] Teague said, ["I agree dear, it went quite well. Let's hope they don't kill each other before they find out how much they love each other."]

CHAPTER THIRTY-SEVEN

The third day after the Tree closed, Dorian and Trevor were fixing breakfast for the four of them when Dorian mentioned a way to hide Trevor's love for Analise from the Dark Man to keep her and their plans safe.

"So you would hypnotize me into believing that Analise is my irritating little sister I can barely stand until a word is given as a cue so I remember she is my true love. You can do that?" Trevor asked incredulous. "Is she even younger then me?"

"I don't know if she is younger, does it matter?" Dorian said, "Yes I can do that, it's not even very hard and no one would ever know you two were in love."

"I don't believe it would work but we can give it a try if you think it will. I honestly do not believe I could ever forget my true love is Analise." Trevor said.

"OK, then after we have all eaten and Georges and Violet have gone back on watch we will do it." Dorian said.

Violet laughed when she heard what Dorian was planning. She said, "I'll go along with it if it works and I've seen you at work Dorian. I can hardly wait to see your face Trev, when this is all over."

Georges was a little more reticent and said, "Are you sure you want to do this Trevor. Analise is your life when you are not trying to save the world. She keeps you balanced well maybe not lately, hell I don't know Trev. Having someone mess with your head is kind of scary, you know."

"Georges, this isn't just anyone. This is Dorian we are talking about here. I need your OK because I need your support." Trevor said.

"OK, I'll go along with it because as you said it is Dorian. I believe he would cut off his left arm rather then hurt Analise or you and it could keep her safe. Besides it probably won't work." Georges said.

"Thanks for your confidence, Georges." Dorian said.

Violet said, "Nothing is going on, we are going to watch this."

Dorian sighed then said, "Let's go to the front of the cabin under that big tree your mom used to have white lights in and a table under to drink tea. I think that would be a good place to give it a try. Georges grab a chair for Trevor please."

Violet looked at Dorian a bit suspiciously but followed them all to the front yard and set on her heels under the tree. She frowned as he positioned the chair just so then she looked at the tree and grinned. She had a good idea what was up and it was between Dorian and her father, they were setting up Trevor and Analise. This was going to be good. Trevor sat down in the chair and Dorian sat across from him in her father's place she noted. Trevor was in the place reserved for guests.

"Lean back and close your eyes," Dorian said. "Think of the tallest peak the sun comes over first thing in the morning and how it makes you feel. How it fills you with joy at the start of a new day and how happy you are at that moment. You are relaxed and happy to sit in your chair and revel in the rising of the sun thinking about Analise and what a nice girl she is. She is a great little sister figuratively though irritating at times. You run through her virtues and faults and realize no matter what, she is just irritating. A little sister who is irritating, you will believe this until you hear

Diablo whispered in your ear on a dark starless night. You will open your eyes and wake when I call her name: Analise."

"Analise, is the little brat back? God she is so irritating sometimes." Trevor said. At Violet and Georges shocked looks he amended, "OK, I shouldn't have called her a brat. I know you guys are her friends, but she can be just like an irritating little sister. Not that you, Violet or the girls were ever that irritating, she just gets under my nerves sometimes. So is she back yet? I would really like to see Hope and how she faired with mother. I know mother loved the little tyke, like we all do."

Dorian said, "No they are not back yet Trev. I thought I saw the Tree move and said her name out loud thinking maybe they were. I hope they are not gone as long as you and Violet were."

Violet and Georges looked at each other with raised brows. Violet said, "You two better get some rest, you relieve us in three hours."

"Three hours?" Trevor said, "What have we been doing?"

"It was your turns to cook remember?" Violet said.

"Yeah, I remember, I just don't know why I am sitting under Mothers tea tree." He said.

"You must have been thinking of Mother," Violet said. "Go to bed."

"OK, I am tired. Come on Dorian, let's get some sleep. Three hours is not long." Trevor said.

"I'll be right there." Dorian said, "I just want a word with our lookouts." Trevor walked away toward camp and bed. "Ok, you two you said you would support me. You heard what he said, Analise is irritating and you are going along with it."

Violet said, "You have something going on with my dad, I can smell it, don't you?"

"Remind me to never let you hypnotize me, Dorian. You are way too good at it. What is Analise going to think when she comes out from under that Tree?" Georges asked.

"Oh I think they are going to be of the same mind, Georges. Let's go be lookouts. We'll support you Dorian; they are both irritating as far as I am concerned." Violet said.

Georges and Violet walked away talking about what had happened and Georges shook his head, then nodded. Dorian headed in the direction Trevor went and to his own bed. He was worried this was not going to work because so many people knew Trevor and Analise. But as Teague pointed out their only good friends were the three of us, it could work if we backed them up. Who would question how they felt about each other, it was not common knowledge they were in love. Yes he decided it would work. He didn't have any idea how irritated they could be in each other. The job was well done.

CHAPTER THIRTY-EIGHT

Analise was excited she now knew where the painting of the Golden Door was. She also finally understood why it kept popping up in different places making people think it was a ghost painting. It was alive in that it had been imbued with a personality and did not like to be hidden, like the Black Sword, a personality with life and force to affect change not hidden under a basket. Those personalities like to be seen and used not hidden away, that's why it was so frustrated and kept showing itself. Though it couldn't show itself for long since it was supposed to be hidden, thus the ghost painting, it was enough to give someone a headache.

Analise picked up her tea and looked at Tessa and Teague. She said, "It has been really nice getting to know you and you giving us your help. I know you were helping Hope back at the lake through skipping stones. How did skipping stones help?"

Teague laughed, "It is not the skipping of the stones so much as what they do. It is a pattern that opens up areas of the mind we seldom use but is very important. The act of skipping stones relaxes the person and allows small adjustments to the mind so that person can accept more readily who or what they are. An adult mind would not allow it but children are more malleable. Normally it would not be done, but in someone so young developing so fast with the talents she has it was necessary. We need to intervene in small ways or risk losing the child. It is a gentle easy way to prevent psychosis and possible self destruction. Your Hope is safe now within herself; you need not worry about her state of mind."

"Thank you so much, she was growing so fast she changed from day to day adding new skills, it was almost like getting a new little girl everyday." Analise said.

Teague replied, "She will still develop quickly though I believe it will slow down. She will be able to accept the fact that say, she gets up one morning and her speech is no longer a baby's but completely developed. It probably shocked you but would have a deeper affect on Hope especially when she would see the way you react. You and everyone that knows her need to accept Hope for who she is. Your acceptance of what she can do and her fast development will go a long way in helping her accept who she is. Keep her on the road to mental health, she will still have some struggles within herself and she should not be struggling with you also. I know you love her and love will heal all wounds." Thinking a minute, he continued, "It was most interesting her mother would not reveal her surname. There was something about her and I can't grasp what it was. It was obvious she loved our little Hope, but still we do not know who she is."

"Isn't there a way you can find out?" Analise asked.

"There are some things you don't do even when you are dead. Prying where someone obviously doesn't want you to go is one. Being our Hope will have to be enough. I feel she has an important part to play in the future of our people."

Glancing up he said, "Here comes our little Hope now with Lily."

Analise turned with a big smile on her face to see the little girl still sleepy from her nap walking toward them clutching her doll in one arm. When she got to Analise she held up her arms to be picked up. She snuggled close into her lap and said, "I'm hungry."

They all smiled and Tessa asked, "What would you like to eat little one?"

"Waffles with strawberries and whipped cream." She answered immediately. "And bacon, yummy." And she gave a little smile.

Tessa got up and said, "Then that's what it will be for you our Hope. Come along Lily lets whip up some waffles. The girls can pick some fresh strawberries. We'll be just a few minutes." She was gone in a flurry taking Lily with her and calling to the other girls. Laughter and a cheerful banging came from the cabin as preparations were made for a feast of waffles.

"Do you think I should go help?" Analise asked.

"Nope, I think you should lay your head back and rock that baby." Teague answered, and that's what she did.

A table had been pulled out onto the porch with a red checked tablecloth. The remains of a meal that Hope declared as the best waffles she had ever eaten lay on the table. Everyone laughed since Hope was only two years old. She polished off the last of the apple juice and grinned.

"Well, it was!" She said.

The older girls started to clear and Analise and Hope got up to help to be told to sit back down the girls would get it.

Tessa said, "Your time with us is about up, you have things that need doing and places you need to go."

Analise and Hope both had tears in their eyes at the thought of leaving this cabin and these people. This had been such a peaceful and happy time and they both knew there was a storm coming and they would be in the midst of it.

Teague said, "Time has turned in your world and events are taking place you need to see and make decisions on how to react to them. It is time to go back to your friends and remember Trevor is not really as irritating as you think."

They all rose from the table and walked into the yard under the tea tree, Tessa took Analise in her arms and said, "I will always think of you as my daughter, know that I will always be watching over you"

She then bent down and said, "Miss Hope you know we are always here for you no matter where you are, remember." Hope reached out and gave her a kiss and said, "I will."

Teague took Analise's hand holding it gently and said, "My love goes with you and my son, be brave and let your heart lead you." Then he kissed her on the cheek.

He picked Hope up and twirled her around, "Now you come back and see us you hear." Hope squealed with laughter and said, "I will grandpa, I will."

The girls were all suddenly there hugging and planting kisses. Telling Analise and Hope they would watch over them when mom and dad would let them. The family of blue eyes slowly backed away from the blue eyed baby and the green eyed woman and as they and the cabin began to fade. Analise and Hope woke up under the Tree of Truth.

The little girl rose slowly to a sitting position and looked around at the flowers and soft glow of light as the branches slowly rose to reveal the outside world. Analise stirred beside her and sat up looking around herself feeling an intense feeling of regret and loss. The soft light from the tree bathed her face as if to say be happy but she knew she would not be happy for a long time. Hope put her little hand in Analise's and looked sadly at her.

Hope said, "I will miss them also and I know some things will be different for you but in the end we will be OK, we must be OK.

Analise pulled the little girl to her in a tight hug and looked up to see her four friends looking in at them.

Georges stood on the left, feet square, tall and strong holding a short sword and knife. Violet was next, hip cocked, hair on end, holding her bow with blue eyes blazing. Trevor was next to her with one foot forward, Black Sword in hand his long black hair hanging loose around his shoulders and for some reason that irritated her. Dorian, her Dorian, her God Father. The tall black man who had protected her all her life stood on the right holding sword and short bow with a worried look on his face.

Trevor spoke, "We were trying to think of a way to broach the tree when it just opened up. My father times things to a fault; he knew we needed you to be back."

"As a matter of fact he did." Analise said irritated at Trevor for finding fault with Teague who she thought of as perfect.

Hope turned around and yelled, "Unca Trev! Then she looked at them all and said, "You are all here and dressed for war, that can't be good. We are here and Ana will be irritated so what must we do?"

Violet stared at the little girl and thought, she put it all in a nut shell and she is only two. She said, "We must go back to Clarion, there has been trouble and we believe the Dark Man is back." She didn't believe in coddling a child who could say the state of things more precisely then most adults.

"Only it's not the Dark Man it's the Dark Men. It's not trouble, its annihilation. They mean for us all to die." Hope said. She scrambled to her feet and continued, "We must go and quickly."

Analise stood and said, "We must warn the people and ready them for war."

"We already have," Trevor said, "We have been in contact with the castle since you went into the tree." Her doubt of their ability to keep on top of things irritated him. "Everyone but you two know of the danger and we were going to find a way to tell you. We couldn't just leave you here." Though his tone said he just might do that.

"Fine, let's get back so we can plan, or do you have that done also?" She said.

"As a matter of………"

"Enough!" Violet shouted, "Really you two, do we have to listen to this prattle when the world is possibly falling apart?" She stared at them in disbelief; this was working way to well. Who were these people who took over her brother and his true love?

Hope scrambled out from under the tree and up to Violet, "I told you Ana would be irritated, for a while it will be the way." She said.

Analise came up and said, "I will not be irritated."

Trevor said, "Let's go."

Dorian said, "We cannot go yet."

They all turned to look at him and he turned to them saying, "The Tree needs me, I must go to it."

CHAPTER THIRTY-NINE

As Dorian stood there with a stubborn look the other five knew it must be important if Dorian was refusing to go when they needed to go.

Violet recovered first and asked, "Why, what does it need you to do?"

"I know not what it wants of me, but I must go to the Tree." He said.

"Trevor said, "How long will it take, do you know?"

"No." Dorian replied, "But I must go now." He turned and walking under the Tree he stood looking up as it closed over him.

Georges said, "That was weird, usually people lay down under the Tree. Maybe it will not take long considering he was standing."

No one said anything. No one moved. They all stood and watched the Tree, each with their own thoughts and wondered what was going on with Dorian under the Tree. They didn't have long to wait. They didn't even have time to get restless.

Dorian stood under the Tree looking into the light and the Tree spoke to him of eons of Tree's and how each generation of humans needs one at some point in time. There is a purpose for each tree, a great need that caused it to germinate. It is a great privilege to carry the seed of the next Tree of Truth. As each Tree gives up its seed to the bearer of its continued existence it dies a little each season, eventually becoming a normal tree just like its brothers in the forest. Time fades all memories of a Tree of Truth to whispers and wonders as it does all things. A bearer must be chosen and a seed birthed for this to happen. You Dorian have been chosen as the bearer of the seed of the Tree of Truth to be taken to a new world because this world will not last. Dorian looked up and saw a beautiful blue pod hanging in the middle of the tree a bright blue seed was pushed from inside the pod. It dropped glistening and the brightest blue he had ever seen into his outstretched hand. This seed you now carry is the culmination of all the Truth carried in each tree down through eons. A great honor granted only to a man of great honor.

Then the branches of the Tree rose and Dorian stood there under the branches of the Tree crying like a baby, head bowed, holding his curled hands to his breast. His friends were all frozen in shock, Dorian crying!

Hope walked under the tree, taking his hand that didn't hold the seed and looking up at Dorian she said, "You will make a good Papa."

All hell broke loose at that.

Trevor said, "Papa, what are you talking about?"

Analise said, "What, what did you say?

Violet said, "Now I have heard it all."

Georges stood with his mouth open saying nothing.

Dorian said, "It is time to go home and take care of business there." He took Hopes hand and walked out from under the Tree of Truth, never looking back knowing he was walking into the future.

Dorian and Hope walked to the campsite under the gaze of their four companions. They started to pack up their supplies and under cover of putting things away Dorian slipped the seed into a small leather pouch on a leather thong which he then slipped over his head and tucked under his shirt next to his heart. Patting his shirt he looked at Hope and slightly shook his head and winked an eye to which she slightly nodded hers and winked both eyes.

Trevor, Analise, Violet and Georges came into camp looking warily at Dorian. Every one of them wondering what happened under the Tree and knowing they were not going to find out. Hope knew something, but they were sure they wouldn't get anything from her. For a two year old she could be unusually reticent.

Hope looked at the four companions and said, "Actually I am three almost four, my mom said so. I was born mid-summer three years ago so I am really more four."

Dorian looked at her and thought this child is going to be a handful. What are we going to do with her? Jasmine can teach her for a while but she will out grow Jasmine soon, then what.

"I guess I could go to the Palace of the Assassins, they could teach me much Jasmine could not." Hope said

Dorian looked at her startled, what did Teague do with this child and are these insights, reading minds, whatever this is, the side affects? He thought.

"It wasn't Grandpa it was Grandma. Grandma said when she protected some of my synapses others would open up expanding and others would come on line so to speak and still others as I grow up. So I seem to be able to hear what you say in your head whether you can project or not. You are just there. I can turn you off kind of like a water spigot but a lot of interesting things have been going on today so I keep listening. We should probably get back to the castle there seems to be a lot of upheaval there." Hope said.

Hope suddenly broke into tears and fell to her knees sobbing. Everyone who was already stunned was stunned even more, and then they all rushed to Hope.

Dorian scooped up the sobbing child and asked, "What is it Hope, what is the matter child?"

Through her sobs Hope cried, "Jasmine is gone, Jasmine is gone, Jazz, Jazz, Jazz...." She could not be consoled and seemed lost in uncontrollable weeping.

Trevor said, "We need to get back and find out what is going on and what Hope means by Jasmine being gone."

They threw their camping gear that they had piled up through the door Trevor opened into the meadow just out side the great front gate of Castle Clarion. It did not land in a pile but they were in a hurry. Dorian stepped through the gate with Hope in his arms and rush to the castle to find the doctor. With all Hope had been through he had never heard her in such a state. Something horrible has happened he knew and they had to find out what and quickly.

Trevor, Analise, Violet and Georges were right behind Dorian and Hope. They could hear shouting ahead of them as they went through the big doors into the Great Hall. Soldiers went out the front gate to retrieve the camping gear thrown on the ground. When they returned Captain Jondar had a guard set on the walls and at every gate. He set double guards at every well. Word went out to the closest villages in the Kingdom for all residents to pull back behind the castle walls. The villages further away had had their people brought through doors into the castle weeks ago. The closer villages thinking they were safe simply by their nearness had waited too long to come. Whatever was going on the people needed to be warned and brought to the castle as quickly as possible, something was happening in the kingdom. Doors needed to be opened even in the nearest villages and the people brought into the castle.

Dorian found the Doctor who directed him to a small room off a passage leading from the Great Room. Ironically it was the same room they had brought Hope to when she was first found. Dorian laid her on the bed and she was completely unresponsive, he stepped back as the Doctor examined her and asked him questions.

He pulled up her eye lids and asked, "Has she eaten anything bad or possibly poisonous?"

Dorian said, "No. We would never let that happen besides she is too smart for that."

"Then tell me what precipitated this shock she seems to be in." The Doctor asked.

"We were packing up to come home when she started screaming, Jasmines gone, Jasmines gone. Then she started crying uncontrollably. We came as quickly as Trevor could open a door. Now she seems asleep but not asleep." Dorian answered.

The Doctor glanced at the four standing in the door of the small room and asked, "Do any of you remember anything else that may be useful." They all shook their heads.

Trevor said, "I am going to contact Jasmine at Heavenly Cart where she is visiting her husband's relatives to be sure she is OK. She went there to help them pack for their move into the castle. She can only send through Hope but I should be able to hear her."

Wrapping Hope up in a heavy blanket the Doctor said, "The more we know the better. Hope is in shock and if we can give her assurances Jasmine is alright it would be good. If not we will just have to stay with her, keep her warm and give her plenty of fluids. She is young and in good health so she should pull out of it. Let's all hope for the best." He stepped past the four in the door and called to a woman down the hall to stay with Hope giving her instructions and to let him know if there was the slightest change.

Dorian leaned down smoothed her hair back and gave Hope a kiss on the brow to everyone's astonishment. He turned to his four friends and said, "The War Room, we need to find out what in hell is going on and fast."

They went to the War Room.

CHAPTER FORTY

Trevor and Violet sat in adjoining chairs and started opening doors to the other Kingdoms. Dorian, Analise and Georges worked the doors asking if anyone had seen or heard anything and warned them to be on high alert. To the Kings they said, gather your people and be ready to move if necessary. Everyone put their army in motion, guarding wells and gates and bringing people in form outlaying areas. They had to be extra cautious because the Dark Men might slip an ally into a castle and cause havoc so everyone had to be screened and hopefully no one had been turned.

Trevor turned his mind toward Heavenly Cart but heard nothing, not one thing. Usually he could pick up something from someone but it was as if Heavenly Cart was no longer there.

"I have to open a door into Heavenly Cart. I have to know what is happening there. It is as silent as a tomb, as if it doesn't exist." Trevor informed everyone in the room.

"Are you sure you should," Analise asked, "What if the Dark Men are there?"

Irritated, Trevor said, "How else are we going to find out what is going on?"

"Your right, Dark Men instead of Dark Man is scary. Dark Man I could handle, plural I don't know." Analise said irritated now.

"We handle what we must and we do not flinch, Princess Analise of Clarion." Dorian said softly.

Analise turned red, and said nothing. Except she wondered what was wrong with her, she could not seem to say or do anything correctly and she was always irritated with Trevor and that can't be right either. Nothing seemed right but yes, they needed to know what happened to Jasmine. While she was thinking Dorian had pulled in a detachment of thirty soldiers to go through the door at Heavenly Cart. He told them what to look for and to do it quickly. Trevor refused to open a door inside the castle and they all went outside the Great Gate into the meadow. That irritated her though it made perfect sense. Trevor opened a door big enough to allow all the soldiers in quickly with Georges and Dorian accompanying them. Analise started to step in after them, she wanted to look for Jasmine also. Violet stopped her and told her to look at herself she was not dressed to go a hunting in possible Dark Man territory. Dorian had paused when Analise tried to come with them, he told her they'd be back soon and then we would all know. Trevor looked irritated with her and that irritated her and her head was pounding and pounding like it would split apart. She bent over and toppled into the fresh spring grass and mud unconscious before she hit the ground. Dorian knelt by her side smoothed back her hair patting her face gently. He then called for a stretcher and soldiers to take her into the castle and to the Doctor. He was worried; Analise did not seem like herself. He was beginning to believe they had made a big mistake that needed correcting as soon as possible.

Trevor was horrified, he could not leave the gate but Analise needed him and that irritated him. Shit, what is wrong with me, I cannot do this, why am I always irritated with Analise when I love her to distraction. Distraction, maybe that's why I do what I do because Analise is a distraction; she is the greatest asset I have why would she be a distraction? Father and Dorian are behind this. I have to stop this before we all get killed. Analise is my true love not an irritating bratty little sister.

He was shouting it now, "Analise is my true love, Analise is my true love, and don't mess with my mind."

Dorian was there, "Yes, Trevor she is. Analise is your true love." He looked at the sky and saw no stars so he whispered; "Diablo." And Trevor fell into quiet contemplation.

"Dorian I now know I cannot do this alone. Thinking it would be safer if Analise and I were separated and no one knew about our love is more dangerous. Being separated will not work, Analise must be by my side and we must be of one mind and take our chances. If a Dark Man tried to take my Analise I would gut him like a fish." Trevor said. "Bring me back my Analise."

Dorian turned to Violet and told her, "Go find Analise do whatever is necessary to whisper, Diablo, in her ear. I mean that literally, push aside or take down whomever you need. I fear the hypnosis is affecting her mind, just bring her back to herself, quickly." Violet looked at Dorian as if to say, I told you it wouldn't work. She then took off at a run for the castle and Analise.

Dorian whispered, "Teague, this didn't work so well maybe we should take a step back and let things flow on there own." To Trevor he said, "She will be herself again soon. I have to go and catch up with the soldiers in Heavenly Cart. Violet will bring her back." He stepped through the door where a small group of soldiers were waiting for him and disappeared into the village. The waiting began for the soldiers return and for Analise. Eventually the soldiers returned with a disheartened Georges and Dorian. There was still no sign of Analise.

"What did you find in Heavenly Cart?" Trevor asked Dorian.

Dorian sighed and said, "Nothing. The buildings are there. Homes, shops and everything that makes a village but no people, none, not one person did we find."

"What about animals? Dogs, cats, horses, cattle, were any left behind or were the animals gone also?" Trevor asked.

Dorian thought about it for a minute then said, "Lots of animals there, left behind. Villagers wouldn't leave their animals behind if they went of their own accord; their animals would go too or be turned loose. So they didn't leave themselves, they were taken. Why? Did they know about Jasmine?"

"No, I don't believe so." Trevor said, "I hope they don't find out who Jasmine is. She was just in the wrong place. They are sending us a message, they can do what ever they want and we can do nothing. I would like to know what Hope was talking about when she said jasmine is gone. How is she gone? How does Hope know? By gone does she mean dead or just gone? Gone where? Where would the Dark Men take Jasmine that Hope could no longer feel her? There are too many questions and no answers. And where is Analise?"

Trevor opened the door in his mind searching for Analise and found only jumbled words and confusion. Suddenly the word Diablo blossomed in her head and she fell into a quiet sleep. He called to Violet who answered.

Violet said, ["She is in the same room with Hope. The Doctor said she is mentally exhausted and needs rest. I explained about the dumb idea of hypnosis and he encouraged me to use the word, Diablo. Everyone worked together because they are really concerned for Analise and I didn't get to take anyone down, Oh well, another day."]

["I will be there shortly, take care of her Violet."] Trevor said.

["What else would I do, my brother? Though I may find her irritating at times, obviously you do not and you need her. This was a dumb idea."] She said.

"Dorian, Analise is with the Doctor and he says mental exhaustion. Violet was able to use Diablo and she is now resting peacefully in the same room as Hope. I need go to her. Do you believe it safe for a group of soldiers to go back into the village?"

Dorian let out a sigh that Analise was OK, and then said, "You want them to go back in and let the animals go?"

"Yes, but only if it is safe we don't want to lose more people. The animals will die if left penned up and I would not want that

to happen. But I won't expend lives to let them go if it is not safe."
Trevor said.

"The thirty that went the first time are familiar with the village and could go through it quickly and safely." He said. "Leave Georges here to watch the door and close it when they return, I'll go with them and we will go armed in groups of ten so it will be done all the quicker."

It was set and Trevor went in search of Analise.

❧ ⸺ ❧

CHAPTER FORTY-ONE

She was starting to wake from sleep when he walked into her room. He looked at Hope who was still asleep and appeared more peaceful. Violet who had been watching over them both got up and said she would join Georges in the meadow.

"Take care of her my brother, and think about making an honest woman of her. It would be good for you both and solve a lot of problems." Violet said as she breezed from the room.

Trevor looked after her as she left, then bent over Analise as her eyes fluttered open.

"Trevor, oh my god how horrible it was. My mind was so messed up and I couldn't think. I thought you were lost to me. I love you so much. I never want to go through that again." She said as she grabbed hold of him as though she would never let go. "It was a devil curse, I am so glad to have been let go of it. What was your father thinking?"

"I have an idea about that. Dorian hypnotized me under mothers tea tree while you were under the tea tree with father being given what I am pretty sure was the same curse. I think Dorian is feeling pretty bad about it but I think dad did it on purpose for a reason." He said

"What would be a good reason to make us feel so horrible and lost without each other. Why, when it made us both so confused." She asked.

"That's why. We know we can't function without each another. We can't afford to be confused. We have to save what we can of this world and we can't if we are mooning over each other. We need each other, and he forced us to acknowledge we love each other and to do something about it. Analise, please marry me. I can't function with out you I love you so much. Please marry me." Trevor said.

Analise lay there with her mouth open and eyes wide then she said, "Oh my, you are right, that is just what he was thinking and he knew we couldn't see it because we were too close. Yes, Yes I will marry you, I love you. I would like to be married in Castle Clarion before we have to leave. I'll bet they let your sister's watch this, and I bet they are really happy."

"I know I am." Trevor said.

"We have to get Hope to wake up. I think the confusion in your mind contributed to her shutting down. Not that it is your fault but when Jasmine disappeared she turned to you and found only confusion so she just shut down." Trevor said, "She is sleeping more peacefully so I am hoping she will wake up soon."

Analise cleared her mind and reached out to the little girl in the next bed. ["Hope, hey honey I'm sorry I wasn't there for you but you need to wake up soon because Uncle Trevor and I are getting married and you need to be there."]

Trevor joined in, ["Hey sweetie, please wake up real soon. We don't have a lot of time and Analise needs help planning the wedding. You get to be in it so get busy and wake up."]

Analise had sat up and they were both looking at Hope. They saw a small smile cross her lips she breathed a sigh and turned over falling into a deeper normal sleep. They were both sure she would wake soon. Then they would help her deal with the disappearance of Jasmine and get busy planning the wedding. Having something to do would be good for the little girl. Trevor and Analise looked into each others eyes and leaned in for a kiss. Their arms went around each other.

Then Trevor whispered in her ear, "What would you say about being the mother to a three almost four year old cute as a button little girl. I would love being her dad and she sure needs parents who love her like we do."

"That would be perfect." Analise replied. "We'll ask her when she wakes up and she can be included in the wedding in a ceremony that we'll create making her our daughter."

A sleepy little voice said, "I already am your daughter, I'm trying to sleep here."

We looked at her and then looked at each other then we went over and kissed her on the cheek. She smiled and started a little baby snore. We tiptoed from the room and the girl watching over Hope slipped in. We walked hand in hand to the Great Room where we found Dorian and Georges just returning to from Heavenly Cart. They had run into no trouble and had thanked the soldiers profusely for helping release the animals. The soldiers said it was a good day's work no one wanted their animals to die because they couldn't let them go themselves. They had left gates and shutters open so the animals could forage and return home if they wished. If the people of Heavenly Cart returned hopefully many of their animals would still be there. Violet had been busy talking to people in other Kingdoms to find out if anyone had any idea what happened to the people in Heavenly Cart.

So far she had found out nothing.

We all came together sitting at our table, the same one we always sit at. Odd how people are creatures of habit. There was wine, hot coffee, ale, rolls and a lot of different cheeses, meats and fruits. We all sort of picked at the food until I said, "Hope is doing better, and sleeping normal."

You would have thought I set a bomb off they all started talking at once. How, when, did she talk, what did she say, are you sure? They all loved Hope so much it was heartening to see the love and concern.

"She says she is already our daughter." I said lifting Analise's hand.

"Ok," Dorian said, "We all know that so why did she say that?

Analise said, "Because we were talking about a ceremony to make her our daughter when we get married and she heard us."

You could have heard a pin drop. Then all hell broke loose. People stood and laughed and pounded each other on the backs.

Violet said, "When?"

Everyone stopped to listen to this answer.

"As soon as Hope wakes up, so we need to plan. Analise wants to be married in Castle Clarion before we have to leave. So it will be.

Dorian had tears in his eyes as he said, "We will have to leave, the Dark Men plan to destroy us. I would rather live on another world then let them get their wish. We will go and we will plan and when they come again we will be ready and we will destroy them to the last of their stinking souls." And he drained his wine glass slamming it on the table. "But first we will see our Princess wed in the home of her birth. And the Dark Man can be damned."

"Dorian, I want you to give me away," Analise said.

"Ah darlin, I would be most honored. Your Dad would be proud of you and the man you have chosen to love. A better man there never was." Dorian said.

"Violet I need you as my Maid of Honor since you are my friend and you stand at my husbands back for which I will be eternally grateful." Analise said.

"Shit," Violet said, "Do I have to wear a dress?"

Analise laughed and said, "I don't know, I never got married before."

Trevor spoke up before that conversation took off and said, "Georges, I spoke to you first among all the people I know and you are the friend I know best. Would you be my Best Man?"

Georges said, "I would be most honored Trevor though I have never done so before, I will do my best."

"OK, we got that out of the way so to speak. The Castle Parson will marry us. When will this wedding take place?" Violet asked. "The sooner the better, I don't believe we have much time."

Hope walked into the War Room followed by her nurse and said, "I'm hungry."

Trevor said, "How about tomorrow?"

Analise picked up the little girl and asked her what she wanted settling on juice and a sweet roll with some cheese and fruit.

Hope said, "Tomorrow is good for me. I am glad you are back, Mommy. We should get married tomorrow because the next day we will leave."

Everyone stopped what they were doing and stared Hope and the little girl's words. Two days, that was all they had left of this world and Analise hasn't told us where the painting is yet. How will we do it all? Panic started to set in, and then Trevor stood up.

He said, "Tomorrow is our wedding day followed by an evacuation on the next to a new world which our Captains will start planning now. Delegate my dear friends and we will enjoy as much as we can. Analise you must plan our wedding while I plan where we will go on our honeymoon, after you give me the location of the painting."

※

Chapter Forty-Two

Analise leaned back in her chair pulling Hope with her for comfort. She said, "I am afraid and I don't know why. I feel like a little girl who saw a boogey man and doesn't want to look in the closet anymore because it's dark. It's in the closet in the nursery in the dark. Something happened in the closet in the dark that frightened me when I was little. We need to go to the closet in the nursery."

Analise got up from her chair putting Hope down as she did, stroking the little girls hair. She looked around as everyone stood up waiting for her to lead the way. She held her head high as if to fortify herself and strode from the room with Hope on her heels and the rest trailing behind. The nursery was on the second floor at the front of the Castle through a series of hallways and a twisty stairway. They finally came to the double doors that open into the rooms the Clarion children had occupied for generations. The doors were a deep golden brown the brass handles worn from countless children and nanny's gripping them to pull them open. Analise now pulled the right hand door handle and walked into a large sunny room with rose colored walls and cream lace curtains at the four windows that made up a window seat full of fluffy soft pillows. A rocking horse stood in the center of the worn round rug made in the shape of a rose. Gaily colored painting decorated the walls and boxes of toys were here and there. A small table with a tea set was against one wall near the window. A bookcase full of books stood on the other side of the window. It was neat but invited children to come and play, it was a magical room. Hope felt it immediately and ran to climb on the horse which she began to rock furiously.

Analise went to another door in the room that when opened led into a bedroom with two small canopy beds. There were more books in cases and paintings for children decorating the walls. A smaller window looked out to the front meadow curtained in lace with a rocking chair placed in front of it. It was very much a little girls room with fluffy pillows, lace bedspreads and pink shades on the lamps. Analise pointed to the closet with its closed door. Clearly she did not want to open it so Trevor strode across the room and opened the closet door. There were some small dresses hanging and a few boxes of old coats and boots. A shelf held small shoes and another held cute hats made just for little girls.

Trevor said, "There is nothing here. Could there be another closet?"

"There is the boy's room on the other side of the play room but I never went there, I had no need. It is inside this closet, I remember clearly." Analise said.

"Inside this closet, but where?" Trevor asked.

Suddenly Hope was there and she said, "Remember the hidden door and the latch, Ana. You know where it is, you must open it for only you can."

Analise stepped forward into the closet and reached forward touching the back of the closet behind the hanging clothes. Those closest heard a soft click and the back of the closet swung into darkness so total that the little light there was, was swallowed up.

Analise gasped, "I was in there, lost. I accidently hit the button and fell in. The door closed and I was trapped. It was so dark and then the light was there. The Golden Door glowed and comforted me with stories of other worlds until I was found. I was punished and told never to speak of the room or the Golden Door. It is in there in the dark and it shouldn't be; it should be free."

The room didn't seem as dark as they stood waiting for a light Georges was sent to find. At first a subtle golden glow was evident then it got stronger as everyone was bathed in its golden glow. Trevor, Dorian, Violet and Hope all crowded into the small room occupied by the painting of the Golden Door as it lit up inviting them in and begging them to take it out of the dark. It missed the light and the people so much they could feel its sadness. Georges showed up with a light to find it was no longer needed. He was pulled toward the painting and held his breath in awe, it was so beautiful it made his heart hurt and he could feel the hurt the painting felt to be locked up. He leaned in to take it from the wall when Trevor stopped him.

"I feel it also, but it is not ours to touch. It calls to one person and only she can remove it and bring it into the light." Trevor said.

Analise stepped forward and said, "He is right the Golden Door is my responsibility, it is part of me and I must bring it out of the dark."

Analise reached forward and grasped the painting lifting it from the wall. It was large and Trevor was worried she would have trouble carrying it but she acted like it was nothing. She took it from the closet and carried it into the playroom. She set it gently on the floor propped up against the wall and knelt gazing at it. Hope walked up took her hand and stood looking at it with her. It glowed like the sun was coming from it. The gardens were in full bloom and vibrant. The girl in the painting was older now and definitely Analise with her green eyes and hair like fire. The door stood open in its golden arch and seemed to pull us in, inviting us to go, where I do not know. We needed to find out where; the Golden Door was our salvation. It was a door to other worlds.

Dorian said, "I never knew there was a secret compartment here. I always wondered where the painting was hidden. I will go find a place to hang it in the War Room so we can study it. I am sure Analise will be able to tell us how we use it." He left for the War Room.

Analise looked perplexed like she wasn't to sure about that. She looked around at the rooms and said, "I had some wonderful times here as a child. We didn't put Hope up here because we wanted her close but I wish she had experienced living here, to be a Princess in a Castle."

Hope spoke up, "I am a Princess in a Castle. You can tell me all your stories and I will listen so it will be like I was there. Let's go see where Dorian is going to put the painting. Can you carry it that far, Ana. I am going to call you mom all the time after we get married? We need to pick out dresses if we are getting married tomorrow. We need to hurry."

We listened to Hope chatter all the way to the War Room. Analise said the painting wasn't heavy at all and it didn't look heavy with her carrying it. If I had tried I knew it would be a different story, I don't think I could have. The painting had an affinity for Analise and only she could do anything with it. She walked directly to the area Dorian had affixed a hanger. It was on the left side of the fireplace above the table we usually sit. It was high enough to not be bothered by the sun, low enough we could see it well. The painting allowed itself to be hung and lit up with a soft golden glow as if it was pleased. Analise walked around the table and sat directly opposite so she could look right at it.

She let out a soft sigh of contentment and whispered, "Hi old friend." The painting glowed brighter.

"Do you think the painting will respond to me?" Trevor asked.

"No, I don't. But don't worry we have everything worked out. We know where we are going. Have everything and everyone ready one hour after we marry. We can not wait until the next day. Doors will open in every Kingdom on that hour leading to our new world. Minimum supplies will be needed but bring clothes. Only the honest and true will be allowed through. Spread the word, any traitor trying to enter the doors will die. We are getting married at 3:00 tomorrow afternoon, here in the War Room. It's the best possible place and time. 4:00 the doors open."

CHAPTER FORTY-THREE

I sat there with my mouth open. Analise did in five minutes what we had been trying to do for hours. Make a plan. I glanced at the painting and it actually looked happy.

"OK, Violet and I will get to work contacting the Kingdoms and giving them the plan as well as the warning. Is there anything I can do for the wedding?" I asked.

"Yes, contact the Kingdoms with Dorian and Georges. I need Violet. And come dressed in something blue to bring out your eyes, nothing formal we will have to run right after the wedding. There will be no time to change. Have what you want to bring ready also." Analise said.

I nodded and turned to look at Violet who looked horrified at the idea of planning a wedding but she got up. Telling this new Analise, No, may not be a good idea. I laughed and Violet scowled at me. Analise took Hope by the hand and Violet followed them out with a pleading glance my way. I just shrugged my shoulders. Dorian, Georges and I got to work. I knew the Kingdoms were not going to like the plan but this was it, especially the part about traitors dying if they try to enter the door. They all wanted to know where they were going. How do you tell them a painting knows and didn't tell us? We just said the world was unnamed and we needed minimal supplies but to bring clothes. They wanted to know what kind of clothes, and on and on. Every Kingdom was the same, same questions we couldn't answer, same concerns and what clothes do we bring? I wished I was planning a wedding.

I finally fell into bed thinking of tomorrow night, or was it tonight when I would not be sleeping alone. Then I thought; it will be on a new world I didn't know. I was angry with myself for not saving this world. I knew the Dark Men had come to wipe us from the face of the world and the best thing to do at this time was run. But it stuck in my craw that we had to run to live to fight another day. We now knew what we would fight and could develop strategies to defeat the Dark Men. And we would live to fight another day. It will stop, I vowed, we will stop them. I fell into a deep dreamless sleep.

I woke late the next morning. What a day to sleep in I thought. The day our world and our lives change. I got up and peaked through the curtain, the sun was up over the mountain and creeping over the meadow. That meadow where I first met Analise and today was the last day I would see it. Am I making the right decision or should we fight? I questioned myself again. I felt sad, then remember I was getting married today and I should be happy. I decide to go get breakfast and decide how I felt after some coffee. Analise whispered, ["Morning, darling."] and I smiled. ["Meet me for coffee?"] I said. She said, ["The bride is not supposed to see the bridegroom before the wedding but under the circumstances I think it's moot."] ["OK, What ever that meant."] I said. ["See you in ten."] She said.

I looked down and thought, ten. First thing was clothes. Then hair and teeth and I needed to run to get there in ten minutes. We met in the doorway and walked in together holding hands. I had asked Cook how she was feeling about Jasmine disappearance since Jasmine was her daughter. She just gaufed and said she would show up, no one goes missing forever. Cook had made waffles for breakfast and Hope was already scarfing down waffles with syrup and whipped cream Violet right next her looking just fine if not content. I wonder briefly if she had gotten out of planning the wedding then thought that was ridiculous of course she didn't. It must have gone her way.

["Don't think brother, it will be awesome."] She said then she smiled.

We piled food on plates and filled big mugs with coffee so dark and hot it burned our mouths. Cook was dithering over what cook pots to bring. She was in love with them all. Breakfast was waffles, fruit, ham and milk or coffee to drink. There would be no wedding feast since we would leave within the hour after. Getting married and leaving for a new world all in one day let alone within an hour, was a bit overwhelming. Analise, Violet and Hope finished and got up to leave. Analise brushed a kiss over my lips before she left and reminded me to wear blue for my eyes.

I wondered not for the first time if we were selling ourselves short. Maybe we could fight the Dark Men and win. Everything pointed to no, and father had said we must go and live to fight another day on our own terms. We knew what they were now; we could find a way to destroy them just not today. I clutched the Black Sword and felt it hum and I could feel its sympathy. We wanted to fight, to kill, and to wreak havoc on the Dark Men for what they were doing to our world. We wanted to see their black blood flow and sink into the ground. Why wait, why not now?

I stood ready to step out and kill; and felt a hand on my shoulder. Dorian asked, "Would you have us die? Would you have none in our world have a chance to live? Would you give none of us the chance to learn how to destroy the Dark Men for the horror they have made of our world? If you choose to fight now we are lost. We all die here and now. Is this your choice?"

I stopped, the Black Sword was silent and I knew it would accept whatever my choice was. How could I choose death for an entire world of people for my wish to fight? For my need for revenge for my family who would be the first to disagree with me and say go, fight another day when you will win, because you know you will win. It was my need to see blood flow and Dark Men die their howls on the wind, their souls sent to hell! I relaxed my grip on the sword. Everyone was right, despite my need we had to wait and learn and prepare a fight the Dark Men would never remember because they would be dead. I reached up and grasped Dorian's hand with mine and twisted into a turn that brought me face to face with this man I had a great respect for. I clasped his shoulder and looked him in the eye. I could see the concern there and the fear that I just might take the fight to them at the great loss of our world.

I smiled and said, "Don't we have a wedding to attend? And since you are so familiar with the clothes I own you can help me figure out what to wear. She said something about blue to match my eyes. After all she is your God-daughter, you wouldn't want her future husband looking disrespectful would you?"

Dorian tilted back his head and laughed, "No, I would not. Let's go get you dressed like a prince."

We went and I believe I was dressed more like a ninja prince then a real prince. It was all Dorian's idea and who was I to argue. I did have a blue silk shirt under a short tight black leather vest that laced up the front with black leather laces. Black leather pants with my black belt with the blue sapphire in the buckle. My black boots rode over my pant legs and weirdest of all was the black leather mask Dorian pulled out and had me wear under my black hat. My hair was pulled back in a long tail down my back and when we were finished I thought I looked quite debonair, especially after I buckled on the Black Sword. Dorian had left to get dressed since he was giving the bride away he wanted to look especially good. Then it was twenty to three, and it was time to go. Where does the time go?

I had taken the opportunity to pack a trunk with the clothes I would take to the new world. I was sure to add the coat and boots that Georges lost brother had given to me on the beach. I dragged the trunk to the door and realized I had packed all my clothes and decided it was a good thing.

I walked down the hall to the Great Room where I was to meet Dorian. I walked in surprised to see he was dressed a lot like me minus the mask. He smiled and I looked around noticing several people dressed exactly like me complete with black tail down their backs. I was startled when I saw some blue eyes and I looked questioningly at Dorian.

He said, "Analise's idea. She thought the more people who looked like you would make you less of a target if something comes up. She had some blue contacts made up for a few men. I agreed and you will not argue."

"That makes all these people a target if something comes up," I said. "That can't be good."

"They were all told the risks, and they are all volunteers so you can't argue or take the risk of offending them; they believe they are doing the right thing. Besides it's fun to play you."

I looked at him as if he were crazy when my sister walked in. She had on exactly what I did except she had a long blue silk skirt that matched her shirt. It buckled around her waist and opened all the way down the front giving her ease of movement and it could be dropped in a second. Her sword hung from the belt and her bow was over her shoulder as well as a quiver of arrows. No wonder she looked so happy and content. Georges showed up wearing what I was wearing minus the mask and the pony tail I have but wearing a sword. The preacher at least looked like he usually looks I thought.

We assembled together and entered the War Room together. It was like walking into a garden and looking at the wall where the painting of the Golden Door hung I knew it was an extension of that garden. The preacher arranged us where he thought we should be when music started to play. I looked suspiciously at the painting but a trio of musicians strolled through the door and slipped to the side of the room. They were playing a strange haunting melody that caught in your mind and throat.

I was recovering from the surprise reaction the music made in me when I noticed a bit of white moving through the door. I realized it was Hope dressed in an exquisite long gown of white lace with ribbons in her hair pulled back from those totally blue eyes. She looked like an angel floating above the ground. I realized the affect was because the dress was too long but it was striking none the less. She wore a loose white belt tied in front with a golden dagger hanging from its side. She smiled at me while she dropped white rose petals from a basket she was carrying and humming with the music.

Then she was there. I couldn't take my eyes off the most beautiful woman I have ever seen. Her long red curls hung down her back like gold on fire and a circlet of gold set with emeralds rested on her brow. She wore a green silk tunic over green silk pants tucked into black boots embroidered in green silk. Her vest was white lace with green thread interwoven throughout and she had a white lace skirt also with green thread woven through it with a train. It was belted around her waist open down the front flowing down and around and swept back. She carried a short sword on the left. There was a fighting knife tucked into her waist band opposite the sword. She was carrying a book. She followed Hope who stood right in front of me and took her place at my side. I took my eyes off her and glanced around noticing a lot of black with blue and green with white on people we called our friends. I realized our people were taking no chances; we would get out alive if it came to a fight.

I turned back to Analise my one true love, and wrapped my arm around Hope pulling her to us. We would be together no matter what, and the ceremony began. Georges stood for me, Violet for Analise and Dorian gave her away as God-father to the Princess of Clarion. We declared Hope our daughter to love and protect as we would love and protect each other. Our names were written in the Book of Clarion that Analise was carrying. We kissed, god we kissed as if we would never kiss again. War does that, makes each moment a treasure and that kiss was the most precious treasure I was ever given.

We heard the clashing and the crashing when the ceremony was over and it was time to leave. The Dark Men had come to take what they believed to be their due as a superior race. Never will it happen, never as long as breath inhabited my body would they take one more soul.

CHAPTER FORTY-FOUR

We left the War Room where the flowers were flowing back into the painting of the Golden Door for the Great Room. Analise and Violet had dropped their skirts and Hope the long skirt on what I had thought was a dress. She had white leggings tucked into small white boots and they all looked like beautiful warrior women even little Hope. The Great Room was filled with people we had brought in from outlying areas. A great cheer went up for Analise and I then we set to work. Violet, Analise and I contacted the other Kingdoms who with last minute preparations were all ready to go, but every one of them took the time to congratulate us on our marriage and daughter.

A runner came in white faced and frightened and said we were surrounded by Dark Men and the people in the villages we couldn't get to earlier were being driven before them. The villagers were in an altered state we associated with the drug the Dark Men used to control them. They were enraged and snapping at each other and you could see the blood lust in their eyes that the drug caused.

A large door opened in the end of the Great Room. It opened into a huge valley deep in high mountains. We all stood staring into what lay before us. There was a herd of horses running in the distance and flock of some kind of large bird landed on a lake at the end of the valley. I noticed strange looking buildings seemingly built into the mountains in the distance. Then we saw other doors opening into the valley with people from the other Kingdoms peering out. I knew we must move and move quickly.

I yelled. "Go, to preserve your lives, Go now!" and the crowd of people surged forward into a new world. The other doors started to spew people into the valley. We had planned having soldiers interspersed through the people and they now kept them calm and moving so as not to jam the area right around the doors. They had seen the buildings in the distance and moved people in that direction. I hoped whoever lived there would welcome a horde of people running from monsters. Hundreds then thousands of people flooded the valley and more kept coming.

We could hear the din of the Dark Men and their servants trying to breach the walls of Castle Clarion. We had opened the Great Doors into the Great Room and people had flooded from outside and inside the castle then through the Door. Dorian, Georges, Violet, Analise, Hope and I stood and waited making sure all went through the Door to safety. Hope insisted she stay with us and we could not make her go through the Door without us.

I could see the last of the people coming through the Great Room doors. Several carters' came right through the Great doors with their great horses pulling wagons piled with trunks of clothes and kept going into the new world. The Drovers were right behind them pushing every animal we had inside the Castle in front of them. There was everything from horses and cattle to chickens when we heard a splintering sound and knew the Castle Gates had been breached. We urged speed and they literally poured through the Door. We had soldiers stationed around the room and they now closed in as the last of the people poured through the Door.

A small group of people suddenly bounced off the door as if there was a shield over it even though others were still going through. The painting had said no traitor would be allowed into the new world. They drew swords and turned to face the soldiers who were moving to surround them. I watched as they tried to fight but it was no contest. They were shoved out the Great Doors as a horde surged up the steps. They tried to run; the fear etched on their faces but the horde over took them and tore them to pieces. Torn apart by the servants of those they would serve.

We scrambled through the door with the soldiers at our backs and turned to see the horde pour into the Great Room with a huge Dark Man at its center. He glared balefully at us with his red eyes, standing tall with a heavy broad sword in one hand his stick in the other. His hat was pulled low and his long black coat whipped in a breeze that was not there. He knew they could not cross the threshold. Three more Dark Men entered at his back all staring at us with red eyes from under the brims of their hats coats whipping in that unworldly breeze.

I looked at Analise and realized she was holding the painting of the Golden door. She was gazing into it and I saw there were now three people in the painting, Analise, Hope and I.

We heard Hope scream, "Jasmine." Then she was running for the Door.

Analise and I looked up to see her sprinting toward the door. Analise's eyes widened when she saw the Dark Men looking at Hope as she ran toward them. We both reacted running after Hope. Analise dropped the painting and it floated to the ground facing the door that was starting to close. Hope had stopped and was wringing her hands as she looked through the closing doors. We reached her just as she threw a blue ball that had a tether through the narrowing opening. The ball snapped around a woman we barely recognized as Jasmine and Hope jerked her through the door. The Dark Men were surprised and looked at Hope with amazement and curiosity. Then the door snapped shut.

The ball rolled on the ground as Jasmine filthy and drugged tried to get to us screaming and scratching, trying to plunge a knife into the ball that held her. Hope let go of the tether but the ball remained with Jasmine inside. It rolled from side to side as Jasmine tried to fight it. Analise and I was completely baffled and amazed at our daughter as she stood looking at her companion trying to escape the bubble to kill her.

I knelt in front of Hope and asked. "How did you know how to do that?"

She seemed stunned as she answered, "I don't know. I just knew I couldn't leave Jasmine to the Dark Men. The Door let her through so she is not a traitor. Will she be OK? Will she daddy?"

My heart broke for this little girl as she called me daddy for the first time, pleading for the life of her friend. Analise knelt beside us and took Hope into her arms.

She said, "She should be, we have detoxed others from the drug and they recovered though they were never totally the same. We can help her but it will take a while and you need to be prepared she may not be the same Jasmine. I hugged them both as Jasmine rolled in the ball screaming and trying to get out.

A crowd had grown around us and the screaming woman in the ball. Some wondered who had let that creature into the new world. Cook came running up yelling that, that creature was her daughter and fell to her knees beside the ball as Jasmine howled at her. We said she was not a creature as Cook cried for her daughter, and we called for the Doctor. He thankfully had thought something like this might happen and had brought the medicine he used to flush the drug from others of the same fate. Though as he looked at the ball thoughtfully he had said he didn't think it would happen quite like this. He observed Jasmine had no trouble breathing through the bubble.

Hope said, "I don't want her to suffocate after I got her out."

The Doctor asked, "Can you strengthen it enough for less air to go through so she will pass out?"

Hope frowned, "Why?"

"If she were asleep then we could clean her up and start the detox process, it won't hurt her if you drop the bubble as soon as she falls asleep.

Hope's face cleared and she turned to the bubble and concentrated. We could see it visibly thicken and Jasmine's struggles to get out lesson as the air was decreased. I noticed the bubble was a lot like the shield the Black Sword produces. I drew the Sword and pointed it at a space next to Hope's bubble and a bubble appeared tethered to the Sword. I let it go and sheathed the Sword. Now I wanted to know why Hope could do it with her bare hands. Then I wondered if I could. Just then Hope's bubble popped and Jasmine lay unconscious on the ground. The Doctor rushed up to her and checked her pulse and breathing pronouncing her alive. He noticed Cook wringing her hands and asked her if she could brew some chicken broth to support Jasmine as she got well. She jumped up happy to be able to help her daughter and rushed off yelling orders to start a fire. She caught a chicken pecking the ground nearby wringing its neck in a quick twist. She then picked up a large pot and putting the bale over her arm headed for the lake and water plucking the chicken as she went dropping a trail of feathers.

He then recommended we tie her in case she woke up. We made a stretcher with blankets and hauled her down the length of the valley to the lake. We lowered her into the water which was not quite freezing and scrubbed her with sand removing her soiled clothing. Analise found her a short shift to wear. Amazingly she did not wake during or after her dunking in the lake. We put the shift on her knowing what kind of black sludge would pour out of her as she detoxed.

We moved her toward the buildings we had seen in the cliffs and half under some trees so she could have sun or shade and was screened partially from observation. The Doctor gave her a healthy dose of the medicine he made for detoxification. Cook came up with the pot full of chicken broth and we forced as much as we could down her throat. Then we piled some blankets up beside her placed a bucket of water with a cup beside them and Hope erected a half dome over her as she started to stir awake. The dome could be shifted as the sludge from the drug was expelled from her body. She could stand and move around a bit. The first thing she did was lunge and tried to attack us through the dome screaming and clawing since we removed her knife. She looked like a crazy wild woman with her long hair streaming over her face. At least she was clean though she wouldn't stay that way for long.

We finally had time to sit back and take a breath and look at our surroundings. We saw there were people in the buildings up on the mountain and hoped they would turn out to be friends. Dorian, Violet and Georges had taken the initiative and there was a line of soldiers between us and them. A good precaution until we found out how these people feel about thousands of people invading their world. Analise, Hope and I sat exhausted from the ordeal with Jasmine. We looked around closer at this world we had traveled to. It was beautiful with soft rolling mountains with little rock so different from Clarion. The trees had large leaves instead of needles and there was a variety of flowers in different shapes and colors. The sun seemed larger and warmer. I saw a strange stripped animal climb down from a tree and gaze at us. It was white and black and looked kind of like a cat though bigger with large blue eyes and big ears. Its tail was solid black I noticed as it turned its back and sauntered away. It didn't seem to be afraid of us at all.

I glanced over where Dorian, Violet and Georges were standing watching a line of people descend from the buildings when I heard a loud cry from Georges. I was on my feet and running toward him as fast as I could, Analise and Hope right behind me. I slowed as I realized Georges was running away from me toward the people and a man was running toward him. They were both shouting and crying and they ran into each other so hard they fell to the ground and lay there hugging, crying and rolling in the grass. Dorian, Violet, Analise, Hope and I approached cautiously to within a few paces and watched with interest. I thought I recognized the man Georges was manhandling.

Hope said, "Daddy that man looks like Georges."

It all came rushing back, the beach, and the man who swam out into the ocean, the grave, meeting Georges the first time. This was his twin Jonas. How did he get here?

They finally got up and brushed themselves off but couldn't keep their arms from around each others shoulders. Georges introduced Jonas as his lost twin.

I asked, "How did you get here?"

He looked at me then looked at me again. He said, "You are the man from the beach who had never seen the sun set over the ocean. That man had brown eyes, you have blue." He held out his hand and said, "Well met blue eyes."

I shook his hand and said, "Trevor. How did you get here Jonas? You swam out into the ocean."

"It's a strange story," he said, "I did swim out into the ocean. I swam in my despair until I was so tired I could swim any more. As I let go of my life and sank below the surface. I realized I did not want to die and started to fight to live. I swam but having sunk so far I was disoriented and I swam down. I was running out of air when I saw a light ahead and thinking I was almost to the surface I gave a last hearty push and came up in the lake. I was so exhausted I passed out on the shore and was found the next morning by others from our world who has found their way here through other natural doors." He gestured behind him, "All these people are from our world and we have realized we were here for a reason."

"Why are you here?" I asked.

"We are here to prepare the way for you, all of you. We knew our world was being destroyed by the Dark Men and we knew someone would find a way to save some of it and they would most likely end up here since the rest of us did. I didn't think it would be you, the young man I watched a sunset with on a distant beach. I hoped fervently my brother would come. We have a lot to talk about."

"What have you done to prepare the way for us?" I asked and I needed to know now; we had a lot of people to house and feed.

"Others have been here longer then the year I have been here. But we are more organized. We have found a way to build housing quickly using rammed earth. There is a mud pit over that hill and we haul mud to coat the walls making a sort of adobe that hardens and holds up well. The buildings have sod roofs and some thatched. They curve and bend and surprisingly it is very pleasing to the eye, comfortable, warm in winter, cool in summer." Jonas said.

Trevor was surprised it had been a year since he sat on that beach and watched Jonas swim into the ocean. That meant he was now twenty-six. So much had happened in that year it felt like yesterday and forever. He looked up and realized everyone was waiting for him to speak.

"How many can you house right now?" Trevor asked.

"Jonas looked at the people sitting and wandering around and said, "Not as many as there are here even if we double them up. It is a good thing it is summer, we can make camps though the winters are mild."

I looked at the people and saw that some were setting up tents and others digging latrines. Someone was taking some responsibility. We needed a plan.

"Families come first especially those with babies and small children they need to be under cover." Trevor said. "Do you think you could house all the families with small children? After them we need the elderly inside."

Jonas said, "Yes, we have quite a lot built. The buildings are easy to build and if we had more labor they would go up fast."

"That is the third step and we have lots of people who have reason to be motivated to build. As for the camps, do you have anything we can make tents out of?" Trevor asked.

Jonas said, "I am sure we could find something, we also have walled courtyards where people could sleep. We could use woven mats as dividers and make shift roofs."

"Dorian, send someone to find Captain Jondar, let's get organized and find out what people have before we have a lot of little cities entrenched in the valley. We need someone to separate out the families with small children and get them settled in the buildings. We need to keep moving, get people settled before they forget why we ran and start thinking about the warm comfortable homes they left." Trevor said.

Jonas asked, "About those work details for more housing?"

"Soldiers, we will use soldiers. They need something to do since we are not directly in danger of the Dark Men. There are also a lot of young men who could use something to do." Trevor said.

"How do you propose to enforce this? Why will anyone listen to you?" Jonas asked.

Georges stepped away from his brother and stepped up beside Trevor. Dorian moved to stand next to Georges. Analise moved up putting Hope in front of her and Trevor. Violet stepped up with a fierce and proud scowl on her pretty face next to Analise. The five of them made a formidable defense.

"Yes, they will listen." Trevor said, "Because of them," and he gestured to his now six companions, "and because of this." He drew the Black Sword and it started to sing a song of homecoming and welcome. They all turned to look at the crowds of people, even Jonas. The song rose above the people who all turned to look and listen to this song of hope. There was suddenly a counterpart to the Black Sword as the Ghost painting of the Golden Door appeared next to them at Analise's feet. They sang a harmony and as they did flowers and trees spilled out of the door and onto the meadow and up the mountain until there were flowers and fruit and fruit trees everywhere. Arbors sprang up big enough to sleep under tucked under trees and covered in dense leaves and flowers. The Black Sword and the Ghost painting worked together to give the people a beautiful place to rest while they made this world home.

Jonas asked, "Who are you?"

The answer was simple, he answered, "Trevor Lee Dawson bearer of the Black Sword."

About the Author

Marsha Lyn lives on her ranch in the mountains of Colorado. She has her kids, horses, dogs and cats for company. The blue skies, wild flowers and gentle winds along with the blowing snow, sub zero temperatures and 70 mph winds for inspiration.